I0689869

Geo. S. A. Vautrot

The False Friend

A Drama in Two Acts

Geo. S. A. Vautrot

The False Friend
A Drama in Two Acts

ISBN/EAN: 9783337343217

Printed in Europe, USA, Canada, Australia, Japan

Cover: Foto ©Andreas Hilbeck / pixelio.de

More available books at **www.hansebooks.com**

THE FALSE FRIEND,

A DRAMA

IN TWO ACTS,

— BY —

GEO. S. A. VAUTROT,

WITH A DESCRIPTION OF COSTUMES, CAST OF THE CHARACTERS, RELATIVE POSITION OF PERFORMERS ON THE STAGE. ENTRANCES AND EXITS, AND THE WHOLE OF THE STAGE BUSINESS. ¯ As performed at the principal American and English Theatres.

Respectfully dedicated to the Arcadian Dramatic Club of Mobile, Ala.

Entered according to Act of Congress in the year 1879, by
A. D. AMES,
In the office of the Librarian of Congress, at Washington.

CLYDE, OHIO :
A. D. AMES, Publisher.

THE FALSE FRIEND.

—

CHARACTERS:

Charles Halliday..................................... ....An English Gentleman.
William Marlborough...A Villain·
Pat O'Brien...An Irish Servant'
Sir Robert Lancaster...
Ben Harris...A Villain—Tool of Marlborough.
Jim Lynx...... ....The Detective.
Rose...· ....Niece of Sir Robert.

—

SCENE—England.

—

TIME—The Present.

—

COSTUMES—Modern.

—

Time of performance—One hour and forty-five minutes.

THE FALSE FRIEND.

ACT I.

SCENE FIRST—*A handsomely furnished room at the residence of Sir Robert Lancaster. Sir Robert discovered L., reading a newspaper. Table R., chairs, etc. Bell on table.*

Sir R. Ah, here it is! (*reads*) "The good ship, Excelsior, left New York on the 18th. Among the passengers was an Englishman, who had went to America to see the grand Centennial." Now if I am not wrong, I know who this young Englishman is. (*looks over the paper*) No news! Bah, these papers are becoming worse and worse. Let me see to-day is the 28th, it will not be long before this young Englishman will arrive. (*knock outside, c.*) Come in.

Enter William Marlborough, c., comes down to R.

Will. Good morning, Sir Robert, reading the morning news I see. Has any great event transpired during the last twenty-four hours?
Sir R. Nothing of very much note. I see that a certain young Englishman is on the way to England. Do you know who it is?
Will. (*aside*) Curse him! (*aloud*) It must be Charles Halliday.
Sir R. Right, my boy, right!
Will. He will be here soon?
Sir R. Yes, in a few days.
Will. I shall be glad to see him.
Sir R. I am delighted to hear you say so, for I feared that owing to some cause. there was a—a—well, a kind of coldness between you.
Will. Oh, no, nothing of the kind. No occasion for any ill feeling between us.
Sir R. Ah! I merely thought that Rose——
Will. Beg pardon, but how is your charming niece, this morning?
Sir R. A little tired. The effects of the ball last night.
Will. Indeed! Can I see her for a few moments?
Sir R. No, and I'll tell you why. She told me she would not be at home to any one, and as she is mistress here, that ends the matter. Call this evening.
Will. This is really a disappointment.
Sir R. Anything important?
Will. No—no! Nothing very particular. I will, as you suggest, call this evening. Good morning, Sir Robert, good morning. (*exit c.*)
Sir R. I wonder what could have been his business with Rose? I don't half like that fellow, but—well, well; he is probably good enough in his way.

Enter Rose, R.

Rose. Dear uncle, who was that gentleman I saw leaving the house?

Sir R. Mr. William Marlborough. I should have thought you would have recognized him, Rose.

Rose. I only saw him as he passed through the gate.

Sir R. He called to see you.

Rose. Did he leave any message for me?

Sir R. None. He said he would call and see you in the evening. I have some letters to write in the library, and will leave you.   (*exit L.*)

Rose. Dear uncle, how kind he is to me. If it were not for him, I would not have a shelter over my head. Left an orphan as I was without money, friends, or a home, everything was dark and desolate for me. I remembered mother having told me of her brother, who had disowned her because she had disgraced the family by marrying a man beneath her in station, but whom she loved. I wrote to him, but it was with fear, for I thought that as he had disowned the sister. he would not recognize her child. But what a surprise for me, when the answer came, inviting me to share his home, expressing regrets that he had so illtreated his sister, and that I should be to him as a daughter. (*knock c.*) Ah, I wonder who that can be ;

Enter William Marlborough, c.

Will. Excuse me, Miss Rose, I thought that I should find Sir Robert here.

Rose. Be seated. Uncle will be here presently.   (*he sits, R., Rose, L.*)

Will. (*looking at paper*) Did you notice this item of news? It will be of much interest to you. Charles Halliday will soon be home.

Rose. Indeed! That is good news.

Will. You seem to be very much pleased, Miss Rose.

Rose. So I am. He has been absent four months, and I am always pleased to see any of my friends.

Will. Mr. Halliday is a very dear friend, I believe—in fact, something more.

Rose. You are impudent. sir. He is a friend, nothing more.

Will. No intentions of giving offense, but I am very much pleased to hear you say so much, as I know he does not care for you.

Rose. (*half vexed*) It does not matter to me whether he cares for me or not.

Will. Are you in earnest? Oh, Rose! if you would only look upon me as your lover——

Rose. (*laughing*) For shame! shame!   (*laughing, exit L.*)

Will. Curse her, she's laughing at me. That she loves Halliday, there can be no doubt, but he shall never have her. I have set my mind on the possesion of this girl, and I will have her, by fair means if passible, if not —well I am not the man to be thwarted in my designs.

Enter Sir Robert, L. with hat, coat and cane.

Sir R. Ah! William, Rose informed me that you were here. How would you like a stroll over my grounds?

Will. Delighted to accompany you.

Sir R. Well, come on then.

Will. (*aside*) I may learn more of this rival. (*after putting on hat*) Lead on, I am ready.   (*exit, talking, c.*)

Enter Rose, L.

Rose. (*picks up paper*) Yes, here it is! He's coming back. I'm so glad. I do like him—no one hears me and I can say so, now. He has never said anything to me of love, and Mr. Marlborough says he regards me only as a friend—but he has shown me so many little attentions, that I—I, O, pshaw! Well I don't care—He promised to write to me, and he has not done it. I think he is real mean, so I do. I don't care one bit for him, and if he says anything to me when he comes, I'll snub him. (*reads the paper*) Yes, he is coming. How I wish he was here now. I don't care to see him very much, anyhow.   (*kisses the paper,—scene closed in.*)

SCENE SECOND—*Landscape in 2d grooves.*

Enter Pat O'Brien, L.

Pat. Och, may the divil fly away wid me, but I'm the lonesomest, an' hungriest boy that ever wer seen. Here am I, Pat O'Brien, jest landed in England from the ould sod, niver a ha'penny in me pocket, an' divil a taste of supper or breakfast have I had. Och, bad luck to the day I iver made up me mind to leave the ould country. (*wipes his face on jacket sleeve*) Bad cess to the mon whoever he was that said: "Live humble, an' you'll be happy." The blundering baste, he niver had say-breeze fer supper, an' nothin' for breakfast; the ould sinner, if I only had him here, (*flourishes stick*) Well, never mind, I must be up an' goin' for I must have somethin' to ate, an' the divil I care how I get it, so I get it. (*looks off* R.) There's a house beyont, perhaps I may yet get a male, who knows? (*starts* R., *stops, listens*) Some one's comin' this way, mayhaps 'tis robbers. 'Tis a moighty foin thing for ye, Pat O'Brien, that ye left yer money at home, or ye moight be afther losin it. (*turns, looks* L.) Who the divils this chap anyhow?

Enter Ben, L.—he is in deep thought

To o' the mornin' to yer honor!

Ben. (*starts*) Bless me—Who are you fellow?

Pat. An' it's long life to yer honor, but I'm a poor wanderin' Irishman, on the lookout for somethin' to do an' somethin' to ate. (*aside*) But more for somethin' to ate.

Ben. So you want something to do?

Pat. Yis, yer honor.

Ben. Let me see, you are not afraid of a little danger, are you?

Pat. Is it foightin' ye mane?

Ben. Well, there may be something in that line.

Pat. (*flourishes stick*) Then I'm the bye for ye. I'd rather foight than ate, so I would.

Ben. (*aside*) I may have use of this fellow, so I'll——(*aloud*) Well Pat, a friend of mine was talking to me the other day, and he said that he would want some one to work for him, but did not say when; so I'll see him again, and if he is in need of any one, I'll recommend him to you.

Pat. Long life to yer honor, may yer honor's shadder niver grow less, an' may bad luck follow ye all yer life——

Ben. What's that you say?

Pat. (*bows*) But niver overtake ye.

Ben. (*aside*) These Irish have the queerest way of wishing one good luck, that ever was heard of.

Pat. If yer honor would only spake a good word for a poor bye, I'd——

Ben. Oh, never mind! if my friend does need you, he'll give you a good round sum for what will have to be done.

Pat. But yer honor, d'ye know what koind of work it is your friend wants me to do?

Ben. I do not. He did not say.

Pat. I hope he's in a hurry, for I want to make me fortin'.

Ben. How are you going to make your fortune?

Pat. Didn't yer honor say that if this friend of yours wanted me, he would give me a good round sum of money?

Ben. I did.

Pat. Then yer honor, as anything round is without an ind, a round sum of money, manes money without ind.

Ben. That is very good logic.

Enter Will, L.

Will. I've got rid of——(*sees Pat and Ben*) Hello! Ben, my boy how do you do?

Ben. First rate, Will, and yourself?

Will. So, so, (*aside to Ben*) Who is this fellow?

Ben. (*ditto*) A poor Irishman, who want's work.

Will. (*to Pat*) Good day, my friend,

Pat. Same to you, sur.

Will. My friend says that you are in want of employment.

Pat. No sur.

Ben. What.

Pat. No sur. I want somethin' to do, an' somethin' to ate.

Will. (*laughs*) Why, that is what I meant.

Pat. I ax yer pardin, sur.

Ben. Don't you think you could give him something to do, Will?

Will. I might have use for him in a couple of weeks.

Pat. So thin ye have nothin' fer me to do at prisent?

Will. I believe not.

Pat. Thin I'll not hire ye fer my master.

Will. None of your insolence, fellow.

Pat. Eh!

Ben. Come, come, Will don't quarrel.   (*Will looks savagely at Pat*

Pat. Arrah, ye may look, an' ye'll not say anythin'; but if I give ye
one with this (*shows stick*) bit ov a stick, ye'll see stars.

Ben. (*Will seems about to advance*) Come with me, Will, I wish to talk
with you.   (*they exit* R.

Pat. I don't like thim chaps, at all. They're afther no good. or me
name's not pat O'Brien. (*starts to follow them—steps—turns around*) Who,
the divil is that comin' up the road. (*looking L.*) By me soul, he looks like
some young lord. I'll wait, he moight want some one—(*looks—starts*) By
the powers he's got a carpet-sack in his hand—Well, Pat O'Brien's not above
carryin' baggage.

Enter Charles Haliday L.

(*holds out hand to take it*) Carry yer baggage, yer honor?

Chas. Yes, my good fellow, I am rather weary, so you may carry it if you
please.

Pat. How much further have ye got to go. I have not had my breakfast yet.

Chas. Do you see that house over yonder? (*points R.*) There is where I
live. Come, I will pay you, and give you something to eat.

Pat. Many thanks, yer honor, but—but—

Chas. Well.

Pat. Wouldn't yer honor be afther wantin' a smart boy, to do nothin'.
I mean—that is—yis—Och, the divil! what do I mean.

Chas. I do not know, my good fellow.

Pat. I want a masther.

Chas. You seem to be an honest sort of a fellow, and—

Pat. So I'll hire ye fer my masther.

Chas. All right, catch hold of that baggage and follow me. (*aside*) I
wonder if he can? I'll try him. (*aloud*) Can you keep a secret.

Pat. (*drops sack—puts hands in pockets*) Kin I kape a secret?

Chas. Yes.

Pat. Well, listen yer honor, an' judge fer yerself. When I started to
this counthry Pat Mahoney, he come to me, he did, an' says he to me, says
he, "Pat, I've somethin' to tell ye." "Ye hev?' says I to him. "Yis,"
says he. "Thin," says I to him, says I, "let 'er rip my bye." "You're the
chap I took ye for" says he.

Chas. What has all that got to do with your keeping a secret?

Pat. Howld, on yer honor. Thin says I to him—

Chas. Well, never mind your "says I's" I'll try you. Pick up the baggage and come along.

Pat. Lord, I'll have me breakfast, so I will.   (*exeunt* R

As they go off, enter Will and Ben R. 3 E.

Ben. So, then, you apprehend trouble from this fellow?

Will. I do.

Ben. Do you think the girl loves him.

Will. Yes.

Ben. And you are certain that the old man is better pleased with him than with you?

Will. I think so.

Ben. The case looks a little bad for you, I must admit. Give me an introduction to the girl for perhaps I can aid you.

Will. All right, this afternoon about three o'clock.

Ben. All right good day.

Will. Good-bye Ben. (*exit Ben* L. 1 E.) There goes a fellow who fears neither God nor man. I hate him; but nevertheless, must appear otherwise, for I may have some other work for him to do, and then——well, no matter. (*looks off* L.) Why, as I live, here comes Charles Haliday. I'll wager fifty pounds, he is just arrived and that he is going to make a call on Rose.

Enter Charles, L. *Will meets him.*

Why, how do you do old boy. Glad to see you. (*shake hands*) You look extremely well.

Chas. Thank you You seem to be enjoying good health also.

Will. Why, yes, never was in better health. When did you arrive?

Chas. About an hour ago.

Will. And out so early?

Chas. Yes, riding in those cars is very tiresome.

Will. Oh, you sly dog, own up, you are going to call on Miss Rose, are you not?

Chas. Well—yes—I thought I should.

Will. I tell you what, old fellow, you would hardly know her, she has improved so much in the last three months. I am in and out at all times, in fact I am rather priviliged. (*aside*) I wonder how he'll like that?

Chas. (*striving to conceal his emotion*) When will the happy event take place?

Will. Well, you see Rose and 1 haven't as yet——

Chas. Oh! I see, allow me to—to—to—(*choking down his agitation*) congratulate you. (*shake hands*

Will. Thank you. I may look upon you as a friend in this matter, may I not? (*Charles nods his head*) Thank you. Am sorry that I cannot stay to talk with you any longer, so adieu. (*aside*) I don't think he'll call on Miss Rose now.

Chas. Good day. (*looks at Will as he goes off* R.) Home at last; but what is home to me now? Home, that pleasant, that most precious of places—it has turned into one of the most desolate of deserts—The one whom I thought to woo and win, has been won by another. He did not wish to give me pain; but Oh! Will, will, you have struck a dagger to my heart, that has dashed to the ground all my bright hopes of the future. (*excitedly*) I love her better than I do my life, and she——well (*calms himself*) she is not to be blamed. I'll not call on Rose this evening. I'll wait until to-morrow evening. (*Rose sings outside*) Surely, I know that voice.

Enter Rose, L., *singing, with basket in her hand—sees Charles—stops.*

Why, Rose—Miss Hazelwood, do you not know me.

Rose. (*starts*) Why, Cha—Mr. Haliday—you—surprised me, so that—I—I—I—

Chas. Miss Hazelwood, I am very glad to have met you, as I was just on my way to your uncle's house.

Rose. I am very glad to see you back again, Mr. Haliday.

Chas. Won't you shake hands?

Rose. Why, yes, certainly. (*shake hands*)

Chas. May I be allowed to accompany you to your home, Miss Hazlewood?

Rose. Miss Hazlewood? It used to be Miss Rose, Mr. Haliday.

Chas. If I may be permited to call you by that dea— name.

Rose. Certainly you can.

Chas. And with you it was Mr. Charles.

Rose. If you like it so, Mr. Charles, so be it.

Chas. I am told that Mr. Marlborough is quite a frequent visitor at your uncle's house, Miss Rose.

Rose. Yes, he calls once in a while.

Chas. I was told that he was a constant visitor.

Rose. He was there this morning early ; but it was to see uncle on some business. (*aside*) Isn't he just splendid ?

Chas. (*aside*) I wonder if she does care for Will !

Rose. (*aside nervously*) I wonder if he does care for me !

Chas. (*aside*) I don't know what in the world is the matter of me.

Rose. (*aside*) I do wish he would say something to me.

Chas. (*aside*) If she doesn't say something presently, I shall run away.

Rose. (*aside*) I feel just like a fool.

Chas. (*aside*) I wish somebody would come

Enter, Pat, R.

and kick me.

Pat. Faith, an' it's meself 'll do that same. (*Rose and Charles start— Rose with a slight scream*)

Chas. Why, Pat, how you startled me.

Pat. An' yer honor would have started worse than that ; if I had done as ye wanted me, so ye would.

Chas. How was that?

Pat. Shure, did yer honor say that ye wished——

Chas. Never mind, Pat.

Rose. I am ready to go home, Mr. Charles.

Pat. Och, the divil, I begs yer pardon, marm, I won't—

Chas. That's all right, Pat.

Rose. I am sure your friend meant no harm Mr. Charles.

Pat. (*aside*) Look at that now, she takes me for me own masther's friend.

Chas. Why, Miss Rose, this man is my—

Pat. That's so, me lady, I am his sarvant, so please ye me lady, (*bows*) and I am his friend too, so I am.

Rose. I know that ; but I—I—I—

Pat. It's all right, me lady, I accept yer apology.

Chas. Shall we go, Miss Rose ?

Rose. Yes, I am quite ready.

Chas. I will be home presently. (*they exeunt,* R.

Pat. Och, but what a purty gal. Och, masther darlin', yez are done for. One look o' thim purty eyes, will knock a hole clane through yer shirt—I mane yer heart : so that a four-in-hand, wid the driver an' meself moight dhrive clane through, an' niver touch aither side, so they will. I know how it is meself. Didn't Judy O'Callaghan hit meself, Pat O'Brien, one look of her eyes, an' where was I ? Nowhere at all, 'til I found meself in the guther ; but how the divil I was afther gittin' there, I cant tell.

Enter Sir Robert and Will.

Who the divil, is thim two? I'm aither thinkin' I'd bether lave the counthry. (*exit*

Sir. R. You astonish me, sir.

Will. I assure your lordship, it is a fact. The poor girl's brother came over in the same ship with him; but he was bound by a promise to his sister not to harm him.

Sir R. I can hardly believe this of Charles.

Will. My friend, Mr. Harris, will substantiate all I say.

Sir R. Where is this friend of yours.

Will. He is mostly in town; but he is at my house to-day.

Sir R. You must bring him up with you, the next time you come.

Will. I am very much obliged to your honor. (*looks off,* L.) Why, bless my soul, 'talk of the—' Here he comes now. He is one of the best friends, I ever had. I did him a small favor once, and he is one of those grateful chaps, you know, and insists on never being able to repay, and all that sort of thing.

Enter Ben, L.

How do you do Ben.

Ben. Good day, Will.

Will. Sir Robert, my friend, Mr. Benjamin Harris.

Ben. Happy to make your lordship's acquaintance.

Sir R. The same to you, sir. Gentlemen, will you not walk up to the house with me?

Will. I would be pleased to my lord, but my friend and I have some business to attend to, which cannot be postponed.

Sir R. I was thinking of inviting you to dine with me; but as you have business to attend to, I suppose that I will have to forego the pleasure.

Will. Yes, my lord, for the present. With your permision however, we will call ab ut five, this afternoon.

Sir R. Certainly, come by all means. Good day gentlemen.

Will.
Ben. } Good day, my Lord.

(*exit, Sir Robert,* R.

Will. I am glad that you came up, because, now that you have had an introduction, you can go with me a little bolder than you otherwise could.

Ben. Yes, although as you know, I am bold enough for most any thing.

Will Yes, you are. I don't believe, outside of those reporters for the news papers, that there is any one who has more assurance than you.

Ben. There's right where I learned it, old boy. I was at one time sensational writer for the 'London Times.'

Will. Then, that accounts for it.

Ben. Yes; but by the way, have you seen that Irishman?

Will. No, I have not.

Ben. I would like very much to get him into my service.

Will. I don't know but what it is better to do without him, for these Irish are so confounded honest, that unless they are pitted against an enemy, they will not do a mean action.

Ben. That is so. (*looks,* R) But who is this, coming.

Will. That, why, bless my soul, that is the young man of whom I was speaking. Observe him closely.

Enter Charles, R. U. E.

Chas. Why, Will, old boy, here again?

Will. Yes, I was on my return home, when I met Sir Robert—he has just left us.

Chas. I have not seen his lordship as yet.

Will. Mr. Haliday, my friend, Mr. Harris.

Chas. (*shake hands*) Happy to make your acquaintance, Mr. Harris.

Ben. Same to you.

Will. Have you seen Rose, Charles?

Chas. Yes, she came along just after you left, and we walked up to the house together.

Will. You didn't say anything to her about what I said, did you?

Chas. No, and neither will I.

Ben. You don't seem to be in the best of spirits, Mr. Haliday.

Will. Perhaps, Ben, he has left a sweetheart behind him.

Chas. No, my friends, I havn't any sweetheart, that I know of.

Will. Oh I that won't do, Charles, you were always a great favorite among the ladies, and I am willing to wager any amount, that you have brought some darling belle's heart with you, across the ocean.

Chas. If I have I am ignorant of the fact.

Will. Charles, will you not favor us with your presence, at dinner?

Chas. I am much obliged ; but will have to decline.

Ben. I am sorry, as I should like to cultivate the acquaintance so happily begun.

Chas. Thank you, Mr. Harris; but it is impossible, as I have business this evening which cannot be postponed.

Will. I am sorry, Charles ; but another time, my dear fellow.

Chas. Some other time I will be most happy to accept your kind invitation.

Will. When shall we see you again?

Chas. To-morrow.

Will. Well, good-bye, for the present.

Ben. Good evening, Mr. Haliday.

Chas. Good evening, gentlemen. (*exeunt Ben and Will,* R.) O ! William Marlborough, I could hate you, if it were not that I love Rose so well. You have hinted to me that you two are lovers. I hardly believe it; but why should it not be true? A few short mouths will change the destiny of an emperor : much more that fickle thing, a woman's heart. But then, Rose and I were not looked upon as lovers. But I— pshaw, pshaw I'll be a man and will not let the world see that I suffer.   (*exit* L.

CURTAIN.

SCENE THIRD—*Same as scene first.*

Enter Sir Robert, C.

Sir R. Ah a man feels much better after eating a good dinner, it is my belief, that under the sun, there is nothing which raises a man's spirit like a good, solid dinner, with a bottle of good old port. I wish that William and Ben had been with me, I do so enjoy company at dinner. To be sure, Rose is lively ; but she was not the same, to day. I wonder what could have been the cause. (*looks at watch*) It is very near the time that William and his friend should be here.

Enter Rose, C.

I wonder where Rose can be.

Rose. (*runs forward and seats herself by Sir Robert*) Here I am, uncle.

Sir R. Oh I you sly puss, listening to me, were you?

Rose. No sir, I merely overheard your last words, and answered them.

Sir R. You like your old uncle, do you not Rose.

Rose. Like you, that is not the word. I love you uncle Robert.

Sir R. Thank you, my dear girl. I treated your dear mother——

Rose. Do not talk of that uncle, let by-gones be by-gones.

Sir R. As you say, Rose.

Rose. Oh I uncle, have you seen Mr. Haliday yet?

Sir R. No, I have not, and if what I hear of him is true, I do not wish see him.

Rose. Why, what has he done?

Sir R. Nothing that I shall tell you ; but rest assured that I shall make all diligent enquiries possible, and if I find that I have not been deceived, *he shall never set his foot in this house again.*

Rose. (*aside*) O! my poor heart. (*aloud*) But uncle, you will give him a chance to defend himself?

Sir R. What is he to you, that you should speak in this manner?

Rose. Nothing—he is nothing to me—only a friend.

Sir R. Rose, you have never deceived me, as yet: do not deceive me now.

Rose. 1 have told you the—— (*stops—throws herself on her knees, at Sir Robert's feet*) Uncle, uncle, I love him. (*sobs*

Sir R. Come, come, Rose, it may not be as bad as I have been informed. I will as I said before, make every possible inquiry into the matter.

Rose. But uncle, he may have enemies, who might wish to harm his character.

Sir R. No, I do not believe that Charles has a single enemy in the world. .

Rose. Oh! uncle. if you knew what it is to love, you would——

Sir R. If I knew what it is to love· Ah! Rose, you have opened a, wound that I thought healed many years ago; but no matter. Calm yourself, and let's have a quiet talk. (*Rose rises*)

Rose. (R.) Forgive me, uncle, I did not know——

Sir R. (C.) Say no more, Rose, I know that you would not willingly, give your old uncle pain.

Rose. But, what is this charge against Charles?

Sir R. As to the accusation brought against him, it is not intended, that your ears should be offended by the recital of such a story. But, you love him?

Rose. Yes, uncle, I love him.

Sir R. Then you would not believe anything wrong of him. Does he · love you?

Rose. I—believe—he—does.

Sir R. Has he said any thing to you yet.

Rose. No sir.

Sir R. Be careful, Rose, and do not let your heart run away with your · head.

Rose. You may rest assured that I will do nothing of which you will be ashamed; but did you not say that Marlborough and a friend, were to visit you this evening?

Sir R. I did.

Rose. I do not like Mr. Marlborough.

Sir R. Why not? He is every inch a gentleman.

Rose. He may be; but he seems to me like a snake. When I look him · in the eyes, it seems as if he were waiting an opportunity to injure me.

Sir R. That is very foolish. (*bell rings*) There they are now: go and admit them. (*exit Rose c.*) So she is in love with the young rascal—that is bad. I would have it otherwise; but what can't be cured, must be endured·

Enter Ben, Will and Rose c.

Ah! good evening, gentlemen.

Ben.
Will. } Good evening, Sir Robert.

Sir R. Mr. Harris, my niece——

Rose. Mr. Marlborough has already introduced us, uncle.

Will. We are not behind hand, are we Sir Robert?

Sir R. A few minutes; but that doesn't signify.

Rose. (*aside.*) I wonder why that man regards me so intently.

Sir R. What is the matter of you, Rose; you don't seem to have any--thing to say.

Rose. (*starts*) Why, uncle, I——

Will. She is thinking, perhaps, of some dear one on the bosom of the deep.

Ben. Or perhaps, of some one, who is so near and yet so far.

Rose. (*angrily*) Uncle, I must——

Sir R. (*laughs*) Come, Rose, the gentlemen only mean a pleasant bit of railery.

Rose (*aside*) I don't believe either of them have any claims to the title, of gentlemen.

Sir R. Come, Rose, you must forgive the young men.

Rose. If they will promise not to offend again, I will.

Sir R. What is the latest news, Mr. Marlborough.

Will. Nothing, of much consequence, only that Mr. Haliday has returned from the United States.

Sir R. Yes, so Rose was saying; but why has he not called on me?

Will. He said that he would have to call on an aunt of his, who lives some few miles from here.

Sir R. Oh! yes, I recollect.

Will. You know she is immensely rich.

Ben. And filial affection, and the desire to please the old lady, which in case of her——

Rose. It is no such thing, Mr. Haliday likes his aunt.

Sir R. There you go again, Rose.

Rose. Well, uncle you know that I always defend the absent.

Will. Especially, when the absent one has the honor to be Mr. Haliday.

Rose. Not any more than every one else, sir.

Sir R. Come, come, you young people will be quarreling again.

Ben. I assure you, Miss Rose, we were joking.

Rose. I don't admire such jokes.

Will. Miss Rose, you young ladies are so peculiar, that we poor fellows do not know how to please you; when we get up a joke on some one who is absent you take it in earnest.

Rose. You will please excuse me gentlemen, I must retire for I have not studied my music lesson, as yet.

Will. Let the music alone for this one time, Miss Rose.

Rose. No, I cannot, so good evening, gentlemen.

Omnes. Good evening.   (*exit* C.

Sir R. Well, my boy, have you heard any more about that young fellow of whom we were speaking this morning?

Will. I have not; but Ben has.

Sir R. Well then, Ben—if you will allow an old man to call you so.

Ben. Certainly, your lordship.

Sir R. I suppose you know to whom we have referance?

Ben. Yes, your lordship; but then being almost an entire stranger to all concerned, I would rather not speak.

Sir R. That does not make the slightest difference in the world.

Ben. I can, then, with all due honesty, vouch for everything that Mr. Marlborough has said.

Sir R. And you can take me to this young man?

Ben. I can my lord.

Sir R. When will you do so?

Ben. To-morrow, if your lordship desires.

Sir R. It is my desire to know the full particulars, as soon as possible.

Ben. It shall be as you wish, my lord.

Will. Come Ben, it is getting late, and time that we should go. (*they rise*

Sir R. What time shall I meet you?

Ben. Say, about nine o'clock.

Will. (*at centre*) Good night, Sir Robert.

Sir R. Good night, Will.

Ben. Good night, your honor.

Sir R. Good night. (*exeunt Ben and Will,* c.) I can hardly believe this tale about Charles, he was always such an honest young man; but then, who knows what kind of company he kept, while in America. They say, those Americans are very loose in their morals. (*knock*) Who can that be, I wonder. (*knock*) Come in.

Enter Pat c.

Why, bless my—Who are you?

Pat. (*bows—takes off hat—puts it on again.*) Och! bad luck to these roads, say I.

Sir R. What do you want?

Pat. Shure, an' its one, Sir Robert Lancaster, that has a purty gal named Rose Hazywood, that I'm afther foindin'.

Sir R. Then I am the one that you are looking for.

Pat. Then this is what I want to give ye. (*hands note—while Sir Robert reads, he looks around the room.*)

Sir R. (*reading*) "Dear Sir: As you are aware by this time, that I have reached home safely, and think, no doubt, that it is strange I have not called on you, I beg to be excused, as I have just returned from a visit to my aunt. With your permission I will call to-morrow. Yours, &c., CHAS. HALIDAY. (*places note on table*) He will, with my permission, call to-morrow. Well, perhaps it will be the last time I will give him my permission. (*seats himself at table—reads as he writes*) "Mr. Charles Haliday, Dear Sir: Your note has just come to hand; will be delighted to see you. Yours, &c. ROBERT LANCASTER. (*folds note*) Here Pat, here is the answer—take it to your master.

Pat. All right, your honor. (*takes off hat, puts note in it, puts hat on head*) It'll go through all safe. (*starts*

Sir R. Look here, Pat. (*Pat comes back*) Where is your hat?

Pat. (*clasping hands on head*) It's on me head, where it ought to be.

Sir R. That is not where it should be.

Pat. (*astonished*) Not where it ought to be?

Sir R. No sir.

Pat. Shure thin, ye don't want me to wear it on me feet, dy'e?

Sir R. No sir, I do not.

Pat Thin, where the divil, ought it to be?

Sir R. You should never keep your hat on, while in a gentleman's parlor.

Pat. An' how the divil, was I to know you's a gintleman?

Sir R. Get out of my house you impudent booby. (*advances on Pat, who exits,* c.) That infernal Irishman does not seem to know anything. If I had him around me, I would break every bone in his body. (*exit c.*

Enter Rose, L.

Rose. I thought I heard uncle talking with some one; but must have been wrong. (*sees note on table*) Ah! what is this?—the writing is familiar— there can be no harm in reading it. (*reads it*) Oh, I am so glad Charles is coming up to-morrow. (*knock*) Dear me who is that? (*kvock*) I suppose I'll have to go and see who it is. (*goes to door, very timidly and opens it*) Why, good evening Mr. Haliday.

Enter Charles, c.

Chas. Good evening, Miss Rose. Is Sir Robert about, I wish to speak to him—in fact to offer him an apology.

Rose. No sir, he has just left the house.

Chas. I am very glad of—that is—I mean—yes I—that is, I want to make an apology for the conduct of my servant.

Rose. So then, it was your servant, I heard with uncle?

Chas. I supp se so. He is an honest fellow; but fond of a joke. He must have made your uncle very angry, judging by what he just told me.

Rose. I do not know. I thought I overheard some one here; but it is of no consequence.

Chas. I am very sorry this happened, because I know that Sir Robert has a violent temper, and when Pat told me of the scene that transpired between your uncle and himself, tired as I was, I hastened here in the hopes of pacifying him.

Rose. You n· cd not fear any ill feeling towards you, on that account.

Chas Miss Rose, I would like to ask you a question.

Rose. (*nervously*) What is it?

Chas. Are you—you (*desperately*) engaged to Mr. Marlborough?   ▸

Rose. (*in astonishment*) No! Who in the world said I was?

Chas. Is he anything to you?

Rose. No! What if he was, Mr. Curiosity?

Chas. It would be a great deal to me.

Rose. And why would it be?

Chas. (*takes her hands*) Because I love you, Rose, better than all the world, and that without you, this world would be a dreary waste.

Rose. (*coquetishly*) Then I am afraid that this world will have to be a dreary waste.

Chas. (*releasing hands*) Oh, Rose, Rose, my darling, do not mock me. If you knew how your words pierced my heart, I am sure you would not have uttered them in that light manner.

Rose. I am sure I did not intend to wound your feelings.

Chas. (*folds arms*) Rose, I had looked forward to this moment with the greatest pleasure—but—God help me to bear it. I may—I am answered—If ever you need a friend, send for Charles Haliday. Good bye, Rose—God bless you.   (*starts for door, c.*)

Rose. (*watches him until he goes to open door*) Charles!

Chas. (*looks around*) Did you call me Miss Hazlewood?

Rose. No, I did not; but where are you going?

Chas. I am going home. Good bye, Miss Hazelwood.

Rose. Good bye, Charles.   (*goes to door*

Chas. Did you say anything, Miss Hazlewood?

Rose. What was that you said a while ago?

Chas. I really don't know. (*she looks him in the face—he starts—grasps her hands*) Oh! Rose, my queen, you love me?

Rose. (*hides face on his bosom*) Yes, I do.

Chas. And I may speak to your uncle, may I not?

Rose. Yes.

Chas. Thank you, my pet. (*looks at watch*) Dear me, how time flies. I should have been home long ago. I'll see you soon, again—at the first opportunity, and until then good bye.

Chas. Good bye, Charlie. (*Charles gets nearly to door*) Charley!

Chas. What is it my love?

Rose Didn't you forget something?   ˙

Chas. No, I believe not.

Rose. You believe not?

Chas. Ah, I see. (*goes to her and kisses her*) Now good bye, little sweet heart.   (*going*

Rose. Good bye, Charlie. (*Charles stops at door, c.—kisses his hand to her —she replies to him in the same way—exit Charles*) He loves me and I have promised to be his wife. Oh, I am too happy, too happy! It seems more like some pleasant dream, from which, I may at any time awake. Oh, Charlie! If you knew how much I love you; but I am afraid you will never know it. I wonder what uncle will say? Suppose he should say no? But then I don't think he will. He would do most anything for his Rose— Ah! I forgot, what did he mean by what he said this morning? I must find out what it was, and I will! I'll ask uncle again in the morning. Oh, dear! I wish it were morning now.   (*exit, c.—scene closes—lights up*

SCENE THIRD—*The outside of the tavern of the village of Exeter—Sign, "The Royal George," "Ale," "porter," &c., on house,* R.—*Enter Sir Robert, Will and Ben,* L.

Ben. This is the place, your honor.

Sir R. But where is the man of whom you spoke?

Ben. I do not see him, my lord. I'll go to the tavern, and see if he's within.

Will. Yes, go Ben. (*exit Ben to inn*) This is rather a nice place, your honor?

Sir R. Yes. You are sure that this young man, of whom you speak, is honest and truthful in what he says?

Will. I think he is, your honor. What benefit would it be to him to tell such a story?

Sir R. Perhaps he might want to blackmail Charles.

Will. Wait until your lordship sees him, then you can judge for yourself.

Re-enter Ben.

Ben. The young man has been here; but has gone again.

Sir R. Did you learn where he had gone?

Ben. The landlord said he went down this street, about three minutes ago.

Sir R. Then we will follow him, as I am most anxious to have this matter settled. (*exeunt,* L.

Enter Pat, R.

Pat. I wondher, where the divil a mon kin git a glass o' whisky. Here am I wanderin' all over this blissid place, an' findin' none. (*sees inn*) By the powers, there's a tavern, may be it's a dacint dhrink, I kin git in there. (*exit to inn*

Enter Charles, L.

Chas. Yesterday, I was ready to curse the day that I arrived home; but now, every thing has changed, Rose has promised to be my wife, and it only remains for me to gain her uncle's consent, and I think I can do that because the old gentleman has always liked me.

Enter Pat, from inn.

Pat. That was an illigant dhrink o'—(*sees Charles*)—wather.

Chas. Why, Pat, how is it you are down here so early?

Pat. You see, yer honor, I am an early riser, an' I thought I would just take a walk before breakfast, yer honor. (*wipes mouth*

Chas. Now, see here, Pat, I want you to tell me the truth.

Pat. Shure, masther, an' it's mesilf niver told a lie, in the whole course o' me life.

Chas. Why do you come out of the tavern, and wipe your mouth in the way you do.

Pat. Shure, your honor, the long walk that I took made me dhry.

Chas. And you went in there to get a drink of whisky?

Pat. No, yer honor, it was only wather.

Chas. Yes, fire water.

Pat. Divil a bit o' fire did I see, anyways.

Chas. Well Pat, it is time we are going home.

Pat. All right, yer honor. (*exit Charles* L.) What the divil moight he be afther doin' down here, so airly. May be it was afther a dhrink o' wather, he was, an thin, may be it's afther a dhrink o'—— (*looks* L.) Who's this, anyway? (*goes to* L. 3 U. E.) It's the ould man, who tried to kick me out o' house, the other right, an' thim two fellows wid him. They sha'n't see mo here. (*exit* L. 3 E.

Enter Sir Robert, Will and Ben—Sir Robert in a passion.

Will. Do you believe the story now, my lord?

Sir R. I do, I do! and I thought Charles an honest man, that was above reproach ; but I find tnat—

Ben. I trust that your lordship will not be too severe with the young man, for your neice may—

Sir R. I shall most certainly order him out of the house, if he dares show himself there again. Good morning, gentleman.

Will and Ben. Good morning, your honor.   (*exit Sir Robert*, L. U. E.

Ben. The coast is clear, as far as Charles Haliday is concerned, if you can manage the girl.

Will. Aye, if I can manage the girl, there's the rub. You say she is in love with Charles?

Ben. I am as certain of it as if she had told me so.

Will. I am inclined to think so too; but it he has not declared himself, I may stand some chance. I had a talk with him yesterday morning, and threw out some delicate hints, which he took.

Ben. Ha, ha, ha! Good—very good!

Will. I also had a talk with Rose, and I took good care to impress upon her that Haliday didn't care a snap for her.

Ben. You shouldn't have done that; but come, let's be going.

Will. All right, come on. We will talk of this matter as we go.

(*exeunt* L.

SCENE FOURTH—*Same as Scene second—Enter Rose* C.—*takes seat—looks at watch.*

Rose. It is nearly time for Charley to come. (*starts*) Ah, a step! I am sure it is him. (*goes to door*, C.) Good evening, Charlie.

Enter Charles, C.

Chas. (*shake hands*) Good evening, little sweetheart. How do you find yourself this evening?

Rose. Oh! I am in splendid spirits.

Chas. Where is your uncle, Rose.

Rose. Why—do you wish to see him?

Chas. You know of what we were talking last evening?

Rose. Yes, I do ; but you needn't be in such a hurry, Mr. Impatience.

Chas. I am not at all impatient, I merely wish him to know what my intentions are, in regard to you; but then Rose, my dear—

Rose. Hush! I hear some one coming.

Enter Sir Robert, C.

Chas. Good evening, Sir Robert.

Sir R. Good evening, sir.

Rose. (*aside*) How snappish he is.

Sir R. Rose you will please retire, I have some business with Mr. Haliday, that requires immediate attention.

Rose. As you please, uncle. (*aside*) He and Charles will have a quarrel I am sure. I'll remain close at hand to prevent mischief.   (*exit Rose*, C.

Chas. I am surprised, Sir Robert, that I should be treated in such a cool manner, especially by you, above all men.

Sir R. And I am surprised that you, above all men, should be the villain you are.

Chas. You will have to explain yourself more clearly, sir.

Sir R. I will explain myself very clearly and distinctly, you infernal

Chas. Hold! Sir Robert.

Sir R. I will not hold, you scoundrel, you viper, you—you—

Enter Rose, who runs to her uncle.

Rose. What is the matter, uncle?

Sir R. (*to Charles*) Get out of my house, and never let me see your accursed face in it again.

Chas. Of what am I accused?

Sir R. You ask me—me, of what you are accused?

Chas. I demand, nay I command you to tell me of what I am accused!

Sir R. And I command you to get out of my house, and never darken it's doors again, and above all, never under any circumstances speak to Rose.

Rose. But uncle——

Sir R. Are you going to leave, or shall I call my servants to kick you out?

Chas. I go, Sir Robert. Good bye Rose. (*business ad libtium for Rose*

Sir R. You infernal puppy, never speak to Rose again!

Chas. Old man, I trust that you will think of this, and one day I may have a chance to right myself; as it is— (*looks at Rose*) Good bye, Rose, I may never see you again, if not I— Good day Sir. (*exit c.*

Sir R. There, I have rid myself of that scoundrel!

Rose. Uncle, uncle! what have you done?

Sir R. I have just sent the most unblushing scoundrel that ever was, out of my house.

Rose. And you have done more than that. Oh, uncle if you knew— (*sobs*

Sir R. (*aside*) It is as I feared, she is in love with this fellow, and he with her. (*aloud*) Why are you weeping, Rose?

Rose. Uncle, uncle, you have broken my heart.

Sir R. Then I'll have to mend it again. I have an offer for your hand.

Rose. And pray, who from?

Sir R. William Marlborough.

Rose. I despise the man!

Sir R. Come no nonsense, you must, *must*, I say—marry him.

Rose. Uncle, I do not love the man.

Sir R. Who said anything about love—William is a gentleman and—

Rose. So is Charles.

Sir R. If ever I hear of you speaking to, or having anything to do with that man, in any manner whatever, out of the house you go.

Rose. (*hides her face in her hands*) Oh, uncle!

Sir R. My mind is made up, either you marry William Marlborough within three months, or back you go to where you came from. (*Rose sinks into a chair sobbing*) Do you hear?

Rose. Yes—I—hear—uncle. (*rises and sinks on her knees before Sir Robert*) Ask me to do any thing that a poor, frail woman can do, and I will do it; but for the sake of the love you bore your mother, do not ask me to marry this man.

Sir R. (*affected*) Rose, Charles Haliday is a scoundrel: he is unworthy your love.

Rose. (*rises*) Who told you he was a scoundrel? Why did you not give him an opportunity to defend himself? The worst of criminals have a chance to speak for themselves, while Mr. Haliday was denied the benefit of knowing of what he was accused.

Sir R. (*aside*) She is too much in love with the young rascal. I don't know but what I might have been too hasty. (*knock*) Come in.

Enter Will, c.

Ah, how do you do, William, I am most happy to see you.

Rose. (*aside*) I begin to suspect— With your permission, uncle, I will retire.

Will. If Miss Rose will allow me to prevail upon her to remain, I should be delighted.

Rose. (*dignified*) No sir, Miss Rose will not allow herself to be prevailed upon—at least, not by you. (*exit, c.*

Will. Sir Robert, I would speak to you concerning my marriage with your niece. Have you informed her?

Sir R. I have.

Will. Do you think she is in love with Haliday?

Sir R. (*aside*) I do believe it; but I'll not tell him so. (*aloud*) No, I—don't think she is.

Will. What did she say when you told her that she was to marry me?

Sir R. She wanted time to think of it.

Will. Well, the quicker she makes up her mind the better. Charles hasn't been here, as yet, has he?

Sir R. Yes, he was here; but I ordered him out and have forbidden him the house. I place a great deal of confidence in you.

Will. I am pleased my lord that you have this confidence in me—I shall always try to deserve it.

Enter Ben, c.

Sir R. Why, how do you do, I had forgotten all about you.

Ben. But I had not forgotten you, my lord. (*winks at Will, who nods*) But I have more news.

Will. What is it?

Ben. After what has happened, I don't think I should speak.

Sir R. What, some more work of that villain, Haliday.

Ben. Yes, your honor, pretty much the same story as you heard this morning.

Sir R. and Will. What?

Ben. The poor young woman is in town, looking for Mr. Haliday.

Sir R. The infernal scoundrel—can I see her?

Ben. You may by going to that address.   (*gives card*

Sir R. (*reading*) "Mary Jones, Potter's alley, third door from corner of Pearl street." (*puts card in pocket*) I'll go at once. Good day, gentlemen.

Ben and Will. Good day, your honor.   (*exit Sir R.*

Will. How did you manage it?

Ben. I found an old pal of mine, who for five pounds, will swear to any thing I wish her to. (*laughing*) If that tale did not spoil Mr. Haliday's chances, I think when Sir Robert hears the yarn that Molly Jones will spin, he will be most completely satisfied. Let's go and take something more congenial to my feelings.

Will. All right, come and drink to my success in a bottle of champagne.
(*exeunt c.*

Enter Rose, R., agitated.

Rose. My bright dream of happiness has been dashed away. All my bright visions have been— Oh, I must not think of it! Uncle says that I must marry William Marlborough, or go back to the poverty out of which he raised me; but marry him I will not. I would die a thousand deaths, before I would sacrifice myself. Oh, Charles, Charles, my darling. Uncle has forbidden you the house—you are not to speak to me. Oh, cruel, cruel, fate! Uncle, uncle, you know not what you have done. (*overcome with emotion—covers face with hands—looks up*)

Enter Pat, advances cautiously.

I have a thought—I will write to him. Uncle told me that he would be absent from home this evening; but who will I get to take the note?

Pat. (*sees Rose about to retreat*) Howly Moses!

Rose. (*starts nervously*) Who—what—what is it you want, my friend!

Pat. (*embarrassed*) I want—I want—you see mam, I—och, murther, what the divil's the matter wid ye, Patrick O'Brien!

Rose. (*angrily*) If you don't instantly leave the room, I will call my uncle to put you out!

Pat. An' if he does, the same thing might be afther happenin' to him again. (*takes off hat—bows*) I ax yer pardin, mam; but I believe—that is, I will be crazy if I don't gather me siven senses.

Rose. (*aside*) What in the world is the matter of the man? (*aloud*) What in the world can I do for you, my good man?

Pat. Faith, an' that's what I'm afther thinkin' about, mam. (*pulls handkerchief from hat—note drops—wipes face—replaces handkerchief—puts hat on head*) I am bothered intirely, so I am.

Rose. You have dropped something.

Pat. So I have. (*picks up note—hands it to Rose*) Read me the outside kiver o' that billy-duck, will ye, mam.

Rose. (*reads*) "Miss Rose Hazelwood." Why, this is for me. (*starts to tear envelope—Pat grabs it*)

Pat. Howld on a minute, me jewel, I'm not so sure about that, I a'n't.

Rose. (*eagerly*) But it is for me, Rose Hazelwood.

Pat. (*shakes head*) I believe that was the name me masther said. Faith, an' I know it was somethin' about a Rose an' a wood; but the divil a one is it I remember. Say that name agaiu, Miss, if ye plase.

Rose. That is my name, Rose Hazelwood.

Pat. (*in doubt*) I don't know whether that was it or not.

Rose. (*lays her hand on his arm and looks winningly into his face*) Yes, Pat, that is for me.

Pat. (*shakes head*) Och, ye soft-soapin' little divil, ye, how did ye know me name is Pat?

Rose. I guessed it.

Pat. Thin guess who this letter is from.

Rose. From your master, Charles Haliday.

Pat. Sure, I've come to the right market. (*gives note to Rose*) Rade away, me darlin' an' give me the answer. Shure an' I'm to have two holidays all to mesilf, if I git back safe.

Rose. (*reading*) "My Dearest Rose: After what has happened, I would not dare visit you again. I write you this, that I may bid you farewell"— Oh heavens—"I must leave. I could not bear to see you, and not be able to speak to you. Good bye, Rose—one long sad farewell. Yours till death, CHARLES HALIDAY." (*Rose folds note—clasps her hands*) Oh, mother, mother, look down upon your daughter. (*Pat uncovers head*) Help me to bear this burden. (*to Pat*) Did your master say when he was going to leave?

Pat. Yis main, day afther to-morrow.

Rose. Then I will have time. Wait one moment. (*seats herself at table—writes*) "Dearest Charles: Your note gives me pain, far more than mere words on paper can express. Uncle will be away from home this evening Your own ROSE." (*gives Pat folded note*) Give that to your master—he'll understand what I mean.

Enters Sir Robert c.

Pat. Och, murther, here's the ould gintleman.

Sir R. Why is this man in the house?

Pat. I'll tell yer honor: I was—I was—

Sir R. Get out of the house, you infernal Irishman, or I'll kick you out!

Pat. An' in kickin' me out you moight be afther havin' the same trouble you did afore.

Sir R. What do you mean?

Pat. I mane you're no gintleman, or you'd be afther kickin' Patbrick out o' yer dirthy parlor. (*Sir Robert starts for him, exit, c., laughing—Rose, exits R.*)

Sir R. What was that Irishman's motive in coming here, Rose? (*sees she is not in*) Why! she has gone. I believe that infernal Irishman is the same one I attempted to kick out the other day. I must be going. Rose is aware that I will not be back until to-morrow, so I believe every thing is arranged.

(*exit c.*

Enter Charles, L.

Chas. Where can she be? Well, I did not send her word at what time I would come. Her uncle has forbidden my entering the house, or speaking

to ber. He hurled insult after insult into my face—he denied me the priv-
ilege of defending myself, or telling me of what I was accused. Some one
has been slandering me. If I only knew who it was—

Enter Pat c.—hands Charles note.

Well, Pat?
Pat. Masther darlin, the ould man's well on his way.
Chas. Pat, you are a good fellow—I will have to raise your wages.
Pat. Many thanks, yer honor, an' I'll accept that same, so I will.
Chas. (*reads from note*) "Uncle will be from home this evening." If it
were not that I have made up my mind to leave, I would be the happiest
man in the world.
Pat. Exceptin' mesilf, masther darlin.'
Chas. Give me your hand, Pat. (*shake hands*) You're a noble fellow; but
where is Rose? She does not know that I am here.
Pat. Faith an' she does, f'what the divil are blinds to a windy made for.
She knows ye are here.

Enter William and Ben, L.

Will. Ho, ho, This is the way my gentleman of honor does, is it? Waits
until the master is gone, then creeps into the house like a thief.
Chas. I came in by the front door. It seems as if you and your friend came
sneaking in.
Will. Have a care how you address me, Mr. Haliday. I am master of
the situation, and I tell you to get out of the house.
Chas. (*in a rage*) You—you—infernal— (*draws knife—advances on Will-
iam*) Draw and defend yourself, you cowardly puppy, or I'll cut you down.
Will. Don't Charles—I am not armed. (*Ben gets behind Charles—raises
knife to stab Charles*)
Pat. (*jumping at Ben*) Howld on, ye murtherin hound, I'm at yer service.
(*Ben retreats Charles turns— William draws pistol—covers Charles*)

*Enter Rose, who rushes between Will and Charles—screams—as Charles turns
William fires—Rose faints in Charles arms— Will and Ben exit
R., followed by Pat, who returns—all very rapidly.*

Chas. Rose, my darling, are you hurt?
Pat. Masther, darlin, did the bullit sthrike ye?
Chas. No, Pat. (*Rose recovers*) Are you hurt, Rose?
Rose. (*faintly*) Only frightened.
Chas. If you had been, I never would have forgiven myself. I ought
not to have come here, after what has passed between your uncle and my-
self.
Rose. You will forgive him, Charles?   (*exit Pat*
Chas. And do you ask me to forgive him? Then hard as it is, I will.
Rose. And Charles, you will not go away, will you?
Chas. Not if you say remain.
Rose. Then I say stay—uncle will surely give his consent when he sees
that I am determined, and Charles, I want you to promise me one thing.
Chas. What is it?   •
Rose. That no matter what my uncle says or does, you will not be angry
with him.
Chas. I promise.
Rose. Thank you, Charles. Now, go for——

Pat rushes in c.

Pat. Be off wid ye. Here's the ould man comin tearin' up the front
walk, wid thim two thaves on both sides of him.
Rose. It is too late—they are here already.
Sir R. (*outside*) I'll kill the infernal scoundrel!

*Exit Rose R.—Sir Robert, Will and Ben rush in c.—Sir Robert advances
on Charles, who keeps out of his way.*

What means this impudence? Had I not forbidden you the house?

Chas. (*folds arms*) Yes sir.

Sir R. Then how is it I find you here?

Pat. (*removes hat—bows*) It's all my fault, yer honor.

Sir R. (*astonished*) Your fault! How is that?

Pat. Well, ye see, yer honor, I was—

Ben. Your lordship should have that Irishman transported for life.

Pat. Ye black hearted villain, howld yer tongue, or I'll give ye a taste o' this. (*shakes stick*) Och, me blood biles so, I'm ready to burst, so I am. (*they turn to go*) Ah, ye murtherin' bla'guards, I'll have at ye yet, er me name's not Pat O'Brien.

Chas. Good evening, my lord, I trust that one day you will find that I am not what I am represented as being. by those two.

Sir R. Get out of my house, or I shall ask my friends here, to kick you out.

Pat. (*prancing about and shaking stick*) Ax 'em, yer honor. Ax 'em! Whoop! That's fwhat I want yer to do. Och, howly Moses! come and kick me out.

Chas. Your lordship will one day repent the words you have just used.
(*exeunt Pat and Charles,* c.

Sir R. What, he dares threaten me! It's too much, I'll make him retract. (*exit* c., *in a passion*)

Will. The last link has been forged, and now it remains for you to—you understand?

Ben. Why, is it that you wish me to put Sir Robert out—

Will. Hush! Notwithstanding he appeared in a passion just now, he suspects us, and with him out of the house, and Charles in the city, I stand a better showing.

Ben. I don't see why you should hate this young fellow so bitterly.

Will. I hate him because he has stolen the heart of the only woman I ever loved, and whom I have sworn to possess.

Ben. I will get him so completely in the toils that no power can save him.

Will. Do so, and within one month I will give you fifty thousand pounds. (*exit* c.

Ben. Fifty thousand pounds is a very large sum for slitting a— (*draws hand across throat*) I never did get such a pull for such little work. Let me see, I'll go and fix myself up as an old man, watch the house, and if my lord makes friends with Haliday, they will return together. When they are in this room, why enter old man with a pitiful story, get possession of Haliday's knife and when he leaves I am alone with Sir Robert, then one good strong blow, and I have made fifty thousand pounds. So here goes to win the money or lose my life. (*exit* c.

Enter Rose, R.

Rose. Oh! wasn't uncle in a terrible passion? Didn't he say some awful things to Charles? But then Charles kept his promise. What did he mean by those words: "you will repent; but then it will be too late"? I am sure he meant no harm. Isn't it delightful to have such a lover as Charley? He is so kind, so good, so gentle. Now look at Mr. Marlborough, every time he comes near me I tremble in spite of myself. Oh, I forget, uncle will not now consent to my marrying Charles, at least he said he would not. Ah, some one comes—I'll retire. (*exit* R.

Enter Sir Robert and Charles, c.

Chas. Why, my lord, you astonish me by what you have just said. I have been rather wild; but no one can with truth, bring such a charge against me, and to prove to you that I am not afraid, let whoever brings this charge against me, bring the person of whom you spoke, and I will face my accusers, as a man of honor should?

Sir R. My dear boy, it does my old heart good to hear you speak in that way. Think no more of what has passed between us, and if Rose loves you, why, here's my hand.   (*shake hands*)

Chas. Thanks : all I ask is a firm friend and no favors.

Enter Ben c., disguised as an old picture peddler.

Sir R. How did you get in without attracting the notice of the servants ?

Ben. Your honor, I am an old man, weary and foot sore, and would beg a nights lodging.

Sir R. I don't believe I can accomodate you.

Ben. Then your honor will please examine my pictures, perhaps you will be kind enough to buy one, and thus help an old man to make an honest penny.

Chas. (*aside*) I don't like the appearance of this fellow.

Sir R. Place your pictures on the table, and we will examine them. (*he does so*) Come Charles, we will see if we can find one that will suit us.
                                    (*Charles goes to table and Ben behind him*

Chas. (*turning over picture*) This seems to be a very nice one, my lord.

Sir R. Tut, tut, boy, call me uncle.

Ben. (*aside*) Ho, ho ! it is just as was expected.

Sir R. Ah, here is a pretty one. (*they bend over pictures—Ben takes knife from Charles' coat, and places it in sleeve*)

Chas. It is very pretty. Look at the expression of that face. He seems to be as happy as I feel at the present moment.

Sir R. I think Rose will be delighted to hear that I have taken you back to my favor. What do you think ?

Chas. If I should express my opinion, I am afraid I should be thought vain. (*to Ben*) How much for this picture ?

Ben. Ten pounds, sir.

Sir R. (*takes out purse—pays Ben*) Here is the money.

Chas. It is time I should return home. As I shall not have an opportunity of seeing Rose, please inform her that there has been an explanation, will you ?

Sir R. I will acquaint Rose with the good news, the first thing in the morning. (*exit Charles, c.*) Well, old man, I thought you were gone.

Ben. No, your honor, I have some business which I must finish before I leave.   (*lays bundle on table*

Sir R. What do you mean, fellow ?

Ben. (*savagely*) I mean that you will never see the sun rise again. (*stabs him—Sir Robert falls—lays knife by his side—takes bundle*) Help ! Murder ! Police !   (*exit R.*

Enter Charles, L., runs to Sir Robert.

Chas. What is this I see ! (*stoops over Sir Robert and picks up knife—springs to his feet*)

Enter William, c.—stops.

Murdered ! Great heaven, murdered !

Will. Help, help, police !

Rose, Pat and police officers rush in from all directions.

There stands the murderer, arrest him. (*officers advance on either side and take him by his arms—drops knife—is stupefied—Will picks up knife*) See it is his knife.   (*shows it to all—Rose screams*

Chas. (*rousing himself*) Before God and man, I am innocent !

Will. Do your duty officers.   (*take Charles to door, c.*)

Chas. Farewell, Rose ; but listen to me : I swear in the presence of the body of your murdered uncle, I am innocent of this terrible crime. Farewell Rose.

Rose. (*screams—runs towards him*) Charles, my darling!   (*fallsin faint*

PICTURE AND CURTAIN.

___

ACT II.

SCENE FIRST—*A lapse of three months—interior of jail, third grooves—Charles sitting at table.*

Chas. It is now three months since that fatal evening. Oh, heavens! to think that I should be accused, and convicted of a crime of which I am innocent. It is too much. Rose has not been near me—she must think me guilty.   (*drops head on table*

Enter Jim Lynx, c.—shakes Charles.

Jim. Come, rouse up, my man.
Chas. (*rousing*) Who are you?
Jim. I am Jim Lynx, the detective, at your service.
Chas. Ah, I recollect.
Jim. Now that you have sent for me, what can I do for you?
Chas. You are aware of what crime I am charged?
Jim. We detectives know everything.
Chas. Then you know who it was that murdered Sir Robert?
Jim. I know that you did not.
Chas. (*jumps up and takes his hands*) God bless you for those words. I now know there are two, who do not believe me guilty.
Jim. I beg pardon, sir, there are three, Pat O'Brien, Miss Rose Hazelwood and myself.
Chas. How do you know that?
Jim. Never mind. Let me hear your story.
Caas. Sir Robert and myself had some very hard words; but afterwards he and I became friends—on the evening he was murdered, he invited me to his house, and when we had been in the parlor some minutes, an old peddler came in.
Jim. What kind of a peddler?
Chas. He was selling pictures. He asked us to buy—we examined them, and it must have been while examining the pictures—for my back was turned towards him—that he stole my knife, which he could easily have done. We finally decided to purchase a picture—Sir Robert paid for it—I left, but had not reached the front gate, when I heard cries of help, murder, police. I rushed into the house, and there I saw—I saw——you know the rest.
Jim. (*during speech was taking notes*) Yes, but whom do you suspect?
Chas. No one—do you?
Jim. I suspect two men.
Chas. Who are they?
Jim. I will not tell you now; but will go and find this Irish servant of yours, and he and I will manage this thing for you.
Chas. Do this and my eternal gratitude will be yours, besides something more substantial.
Jim. Thank you. Good day.
Chas. Good day. (*exit Lynx,* R.) Oh, God! I thank Thee for having given me two true friends—and Rose—that man said she did not believe me guilty. Why is it then that she has not been to see me?

Enter Will, L.

Will. Good morning, Mr. Haliday, have you heard any news lately?
Chas. No, I have not.
Will. Never mind, I have a proposition to make, to which, if you con-

sent, you will not only save your life, but you will regain your liberty.
You are aware that murder is a crime punishable by death?

Chas. Yes; but my sentence was——

Will. Imprisonment for life; but how long do you suppose you could
live in this place?

Chas. Ah! not long. I am already feeling weak and faint; but your
proposition?

Will. It is this: you know I am rich and have great influence. Promise me that if I succeed in opening your prison doors, you will leave the
country.

Chas. And Rose?

Will. You must not see her.

Chas. Then I will not——

Will. Rose believes you guilty of murdering her father.

Chas. You lie, villain that you are!

Will. If I was not master of the situation, I would not take your insults
so tamely. Then you refuse my offer?

Chas. I do.

Will. Then listen: you will die the death of a dog. Money is all power-
ful, and can do many things in a bold man's hands. After you have ceased
to inhabit this beautiful world, I shall marry Rose, and——

Chas. (*starts towards him*) You infernal——

Will. (*points pistol*) Keep off, or I will shoot you. And after we are mar-
ried, we will sometimes talk about poor Charles Haliday, who was hung
for—— (*Charles jumps on him—they struggle—Will drops pistol—Charles
throws him down*) Help, murder, murder!

Jim and Pat rush in R., and take Charles off Will.

Jim. You must not do this, Mr. Haliday.

Pat Och, yer murtherin' thafe, an' if I had known 'twas you, I would
have helped me masther sthrangle the life out o' ye. (*Charles s ts in chair
with head on table*) Och, me poor masther.

Jim. Come, Mr. Haliday, cheer up.

Will. I shall have a——

Pat. (*advancing*) Now look a here: the best thing ye can do is to git out
o' here, before I can say Jack Robinson.

Will. I will go; but I shall call upon you as a witness of this assault.
Mr. Haliday, you shall hear from me again.　　　　(*exit, L.*)

Jim. What is this fellows name, Mr. Haliday?

Chas. William Marlborough. (*Lynx starts*) You seem surprized.

Jim. Do I? (*aside*) Whew! I know my men now. (*aloud*) Well, Mr.
Haliday, we have a proposition to make to you. We propose to effect your
escape.

Chas. And let the world think that I am guilty, and am——　　　　＇

Jim. The world thinks you are guilty anyhow.

Chas. Well, let me hear your plan.

Jim. Our plan is simply to fix you up so your own mother wouldn't
know you, and then we will have three working, instead of two.

Chas. I consent. When will you make the attempt?

Jim. As soon as possible.

Chas. May heaven aid you and grant you success.

Jim. Well, we must go, so that we can commence our work. Good bye,
Mr. Haliday. Keep a stout heart.

Pat. Good bye, masther, darlin.

Chas. Good bye, my friends. (*shakes hands*) I hope soon to see this mystery cleared up. (*exit Lynx and Pat, R.*) Heaven has heard my prayers, and
sent me a friend, when I least expected one. Oh, Rose, Rose! how I long
to be with you, so that I may watch your enemies, and mine. Can it be
that William Marlborough is implicated? I begin to suspect him. Let

him look to himself if my suspicions should prove correct, for my vengeance will be terrible. *(sits at table—scene closes*

—————

SCENE SECOND—*Interior of tavern at the village—Bar, back, with shelves, bottles, etc.—Tables* C. *of stage, with chairs. Lynx as bar-keeper—disguised.*

Jim. Fortune favors me. From conversation I overheard between those two men, I learned they would be here, and something was said about a large sum of money due Harris. Feeling sure that it was somehow connected with the murder of Sir Robert, I determined to be ready for them. The landlord of this inn, is an old friend of mine, and readily consented to the arrangement, and Jim Lynx is duly installed, for a short time at least, in his stead. But, hark ! some one is coming. I am very deaf.

Enter Ben and Will, C.

Ben. *(loudly)* I sry, lai dlord.
Jim. Aye, aye, sir.
Ben. Look lively, and bring us a bottle of your best wine.
Jim. Aye, aye, sir. Here's your wine, gentlemen. *(places wine and glasses on table)*
Ben. Come fill up. *(fill glasses)* Here's luck to you.
Will. Thank you. *(they drink)* You do not feel quite as nervous as you did ?
Ben. I must say that I do not.
Will. Then let me hear how you—— *(Ben points to Jim)* I say, landlord. *(moderately—Jim does not hear)* Landlord ! Landlord ! *(does not hear—louder)* I say, landlord !
Jim. *(starts—during the conversation, was cleaning glasses)* Eh, what did you say, gentlemen ?
Will. He can't hear, so proceed.
Ben. All right, here goes. *(Pat sings outside)* Who is that ?
Will. It sounds like that Irishman's voice.

Enter Pat, C.

Pat. Helloa—hic—Mr. Landlord—hic—I want a—hic dhrink. *(staggers to table where Ben and Will are)*
Jim. You have had too much, already, and I'll not give you any more. *(aside)* He'll spoil the whole business.
Will. *(aside to Ben)* Let's fill him full, and then pump him dry.
Ben. *(aside to Will)* All right. *(to Pat)* Here my friend, here's a glass of wine. *(gives Pat glass*
Pat. Many thanks. I am—hic—Pathrick O—hic—Brien, at yer—hic—sarvice. *(drinks—sets glass down*
Will. I say, Pat, when——
Pat. Eh, so it is—hic—ye are the—hic—chaps that masther—hic——
Will. I forgive him, and I also forgive you for the words you used. *(Jim catches hold of Pat)*
Jim. You must get out of this. I can't have any drunken men here.
Pat. Howld on, yer—hic—honor, I'm not dhrunk—I'm——
Ben. Let him alone, landlord , we'll answer for him.
Will. Come, Pat, sit down. *(Ben sits,* R. *of table, Will* L., *Pat.,* C.—*Jim very much annoyed)*
Pat. *(pours out wine)* This is the foinest—hic—liquor that I ever tasted. *(presents glass)* Here's long life to yer—hic—honor.
Ben. Thank you ; but see here, Pat, they tell me that your master is innocent of the crime with which he is charged.
Pat. *(shakes ffst)* An' so he—hic—is— don't yer—hic—believe it ?
Ben. The evidence was strong against him.
Pat. I don't believe—hic—he murthered the old—hic—man.

Will. But who could have done it?
Pat. Au' that's just f'what I—hic——   (*Jim drops glass*)
Ben. (*loud voice*) What's the matter landlord?
Jim. Dropped a glass.
Ben. You was about to say, Pat, that——
Pat. I would loik a—hic—nother dbrink.
Will. Give him what's left, Ben.   (*Ben gives wine—Pat drinks*)
Will. Well, who is it you suspect?
Pat. Sus—pect? Who the—hic—divil arc ye—hic—talking about? I—hic—don't owe—hic—him any—hic—thing. Landlord—hic— (*Jim runs to him*) do ye—hic—mane to say—hic—that I—hic—owe ye—hic—any-thing?   (*leans head on table*)
Jim. No, who said you did?
Pat. No, an' I'll—hic—not go—hic—home. I'll stay—hic—here. (*rolls off chair—motions to Jim*)
Jim. (*aside to Pat*) Are you playing 'possum, Pat?
Pat. (*aside to Jim*) An' I'm a grane 'possum, so I am?
Jim. Gentlemen, if you wish anything, call and I'll attend to you. (*goes behind bar—arranges things*)
Will. That last drink you gave him was too much, Ben.
Ben. Here Pat, get up. (*shakes him with foot*) You would have to shoot a cannon over him to wake him now.
Will. I am glad, for we have been interrupted so many times, that I have almost despaired of hearing your story.
Ben. (*looks at Pat and Jim—Jim is whistling*) Well here is the story: I dressed myself as an old picture dealer. Here landlord quit that infernal whistling!
Jim. Beg pardon, your honor, didn't mean any harm.
Ben. I fixed myself up as an old picture dealer, and hung around the house, watching my chance. It was just as you thought, they had made friends. I followed them into the house, and implored them to buy a pic-ture. (*Pat takes folded paper from Ben's pocket and puts it in his own*) They examined the pictures and while they were looking at them, I stole Hali-day's knife.
Pat. Och, murther!   (*Ben and Will start—Jim looks up*)
Will. What was that?
Ben. This infernal Irishman. I say Pat.   (*shakes him with foot*)
Will. I had forgotten him—go on.
Ben. They finally selected a picture, paid for it, and Haliday left. As soon as I thought he was out of reach, why I—— Well, you know what happened.
Jim. (*aside*) Right sharp, it was.
Ben. Here landlord! (*Ben goes to table*) How much do we owe you?
Jim. Eight shillings.
Will. (*gives money*) We shall patronize you very often. (*exeunt, c.—as they go Pat goes to Jim and they shake hands*)
Pat. Thought I was dhrunk, did ye? Och, ye're not shmart, at all.
Jim. I really did think you was drunk.
Pat. Faith an' I know ye did; but look here. (*gives Jim paper*) rade this.
Jim. (*glances at it*) Ha, ha, ha!
Pat. (*in amazement*) Listen. "London, July 10th. For and in considera-tion of a certain piece of work, to be performed by Benjamin Harris, I, the undersigned, do hereby promise to pay, three months after date, the sum of fifty thousand pounds, provided said work is satisfactorily done. Signed; WILLIAM MARLBOROUGH." Here is another one. "I, the undersigned, prom-ise, in consideration of the sum named in the foregoing paper, to faithfully perform the said work, and to deliver up this contract to the said William Marlborough, on the payment of the said fifty thousand pounds. Signed. BENJAMIN HARRIS." Where in the world did you find this paper, Pat?

Pat. In the coat pocket of that——

Enter Ben, hurriedly.

Exactly, f'what I—hic—say, an' f'what are ye—hic—going to—hic—do about it? *(Jim hides paper*

Ben. I say, landlord, you didn't see a piece of paper on the floor, did you?

Jim. (*looks around table*) No sir, I did not.

Ben. If any one should find it, I would be ruined. It is a receipt for a large amount, which I have paid, and I do not like to trust the man.

Jim. I haven't seen it, your honor.

Ben. I am very sorry. *(exit C.*

Pat. Faith, but that was a close shave.

Jim. So it was; but come, we must be on the track of those fellows. I'll go and tell the landlord to take posession; but by the way, is everything arranged for Haliday's escape?

Pat. Yis, ivery thing is ready.

Jim. Well then, remember eleven o'clock to-night. At twelve we will try.

Pat. I'm there ivery time. *(exeunt C.—scene closes*

––––––

SCENE THIRD—*Landscape, second grooves—Enter Will and Ben, talking as they cross stage.*

Will. Are you sure that you did not lose that paper, Ben?

Ben. Yes, I am certain.

Will. All right, I'll take your word for it. *(exeunt, R.*

Enter Pat and Jim.

Jim. Didn't that chap look blue, Pat?

Pat. I'm afther thinkin' it's bilious, he looked.

Jim. Ha, ha, ha! That was a cute trick of yours.

Pat. Yis, I thought I'd steal somethin' from him, bekase he put his dirthy foot on me. *(examines and brushes coat*

Jim. So you just wanted to get even with him?

Pat. An' it's I thats afther thirkin I don't owe him anythin'.

Jim. We are all right now. All we want is to find the disguise he wore, and to get Charles out of prison. You are ready for to-night—you know the signal?—three whistles.

Pat. Yis, I know 'em.

Jim. What are you to do when you hear me whistle?

Pat. Whin ye whistles the third time, I'm to throw a bit o' a pebble into me masther's cell. The pebble is to be tied to a sthring—the sthring to a rope, and——

Jim. All right. I must go now. Don't fail. *(exit L.*

Pat. An' it's me ye're afther axin not to fail? By all the blood o' me four fathers, eight mothers an' siventeen gran'mothers, I'll not fail ye! *(exit B.—scene closes*

––––––

SCENE FOURTH—*Prison—Charles rises and walks about, goes to window,* L., *tries bars, listens.*

Chas. The bars are all sawed through; but what an awful height. There goes the quarter. In a few minutes it will be twelve o'clock and then—— (*whistle heard*) There is the first signal—my friends have not failed me. Ah what is that—a man on the top of the house, creeping slowly along—it is Pat—the faithful fellow is risking his life for me. (*whistle heard*) There is the second signal. See how reckless Pat is moving—he will fall. Oh, heaven! (*coverseyes—looks*) No, he is all right, again. See, he is now within—— (*in a whisper*) Pat, Pat. (*whistle—clock begins to strike—Charles leaves window—pebble falls—picks it up and follows string to window and draws up rope—gets on table and breaks bars—fastens rope on opposite side of stage—uncovers head and turns eyes to heaven*) Oh, God, in thy hands I place my life. (*climbs out window*

Enter William, R.

Will. (*cuts rope which disappears rapidly*) Thus have I my revenge. (*scene closes*)

———

SCENE FIFTH—*Landscape—Enter Pat, L.*

Pat. Sure an' I had a narrer escape. I dhropped right on the head of a cop, as he wus passin'. I woudher if master got away. I seen him git out o' the windy, an' thin I couldn't see him any more; but it seems to me I heard a sthrange noise. Faith, it frightened me. I wondher where the divil that detective is, any way! (*looks off L.*) Ah, here he comes.

Enter Jim, L,

Bad luck to yer lazy bones. Why the divil did ye kape me waitin' so long?
Jim. (*dolefully*) Aye, and it's bad luck sure enough.
Pat. Anythin' gone wrong?
Jim. Yes, poor Mr. Haliday——
Pat. (*excitedly*) Tell me, didn't me masther git away all right?
Jim. He had got about half way down, when some one cut the rope, and he fell down to the——
Pat. To the ground, an' was kilt intirely?
Jim. No.
Pat. No? Tell me the truth, or I'll murther ye?
Jim. Well, he is all right. You shall hear the tale from his own lips.
Pat. Come on, bring me to him. (*starts R.—stops*) Och, murther!
Jim. What's the matter, Pat?
Pat. Look there. (*points R.*
Jim. Ah, I see. We had better not be seen together, so 'au revoir,' as the French say. (*exit, R.*
Pat. To the divil wid ye, an' yer Frinch sayin's. Dont be afther come-in' any o' yer frog-atin' spaches over me.

Enter Will, R.

Will. So at last he is out of the way, and in a manner that will bring credit upon myself, although I shall take very good care not to let it be known that I was implicated. (*sees Pat*) Why, how do you do, Pat?
Pat. Pretty well, thank ye, without ye.
Will. Shut up, and don't give me any of your lip.
Pat. An shure, if I was to give a piece of my lip, ye'd have more than ye could carry.
Will. I'll break every bone in your body, you——
Pat. An' that's just i'what ye'd bether not be afther tryin', so it is. (*shakes stick*
Will. Come, come, Pat, think nothing of what I have said. Let's be friends.
Pat. All right, if I've said anythin that I'm sorry for. I'm glad of it.
Will. Why——(*checks himself*) I believe Miss Rose wants you, Pat.
Pat. Thin I'll go, an' small thanks to yer, for the same. (*exit, R.*
Will. I am afraid that Irishman will prove troublesome; but never mind. (*whistle outside*) Ah that is Ben—he promised to bring that agreement with him.

Enter Ben L.

You are punctual, Ben. You have brought the agreement?

Ben. Yes, here it is.

Will. (*bu n p per*) Thus do I destroy every vestage of the 'crime.

Ben. (*a i e*) If he had looked inside, he would have seen that it was a blank—the original I have l st.

Will. Ashes never tell tales, do they Ben?

Ben. No, they are like dead men, they never mount a witness box.

Chas. (*outside in deep hollow voice*) But there will be one who will. (*Ben and Will look at each other in horror—business ad libitum*)

Will. What was that?

Ben. I do not know.

Will. Very mysterious!

Ben. Come. (*Will draws knife, Ben a pistol—exit* L.

Enter Charles, disguised as old man.

Chas. Ah I gave them a good scare, at least. They were the worst frightened men that I have seen in many a day; but where can that detective be. He promised to be here by this time. There must be something detaining him, for he is usually punctual. (*Pat sings*) Ah, that is Pat's voice—I'll see if he knows me.

Enter Pat, R.

Good morning, my friend.

Pat. Same to you sir. (*aside*) Who the divil's this ould rooster, anyway?

Chas. You don't happen to know, nobody who wants a good gardener, do you?

Pat. Yis sir.

Chas. Then perhaps you would not object to tell me who it is?

Pat. No sir, I haven't the least objection in the wourld. Are ye a good gardener?

Chas. I am.

Pat. I nade a mon to help me.

Chas. Then I am the one.

Pat. Ye are too ould, mon.

Chas. That is nothing against me if I do your work, is it?

Pat. No, an' I belave I'll hire ye.

Chas. Are you acquainted with one, Charles Haliday, who lives about here?

Pat. I was; but he's gone dead—long life to him.

Chas. I was a friend of his father. and would like to know something of his son.

Pat. An' shure, ye haven't inthroduced yersilf, as yet.

Chas. My name is Andrew Hobart.

Pat. An' mine is——

Chas. Patrick O'Brien.

Pat. (*astonished*) How did you know that?

Chas. I know it. and that is sufficient.

Pat. An' shure, ye're the divil's own brother. Well, misther Hobart, I think I'll try ye one month, on trial.

Chas. What do you pay by the month?

Pat. The last mon I had, I gave him nothing the first month, and the second month I gave him one square male. At the ind o' the month he did'nt like it, so he left.

Chas. Well, what will ye give me?

Pat. I'll give ye a square male once a wake, an tin cints on Sunday.

Chas. But leaving all jokes aside, do you really want a man to help you, and if so, what will you give?

Pat. I'll give you lodging, three males a day an' tin dollars a month.

Chas. I'll take the place.

Pat. You're a sensible ould mon, an I'll hire ye, so come 'long wid me.

Chas. I cannot go at present, for I have an appointment with a friend. Ah, here he comes now.

Pat.   An' by me soul, but it's Jim Lynx the detective.

Enter Jim, R.

Jim.   Ah, good morning, Mr.— (*Charles puts finger on lips*) Hobart, I am sorry that I have kept you waiting?

Chas.   It is of no consequence. How are things progressing, Mr. Lynx?

Jim.   Capital, capital!

Pat. (*aside*) I smell a mice, an' it's a great big one.

Jim.   I say Pat, you haven't seen anything of those two fellows, have you?

Pat.   Yis, I seen the big one, an, he woer about to punch me head.

Jim.   He was?

Pat.   Yis; but we made friends, afther a manner.

Chas. (*natural voice*) That's just like the infernal——

Pat. (*jumps*) Faith, an' I know ye now, masther darlin'. Och, murther! yer own mither wouldn't a known ye, in that rig.

Chas.   It remains now to be seen whether Rose will know me. So you'll hire me, will you not, Mr. O'Brien?

Pat.   I ax yer pardin, masther darlin, I wor only jokin'.

Chas.   Come, friends, I am anxious to see her.

Jim.   Well, come on, for I wish to become well acquainted with the ne ghborhood.

Pat   Come on thin, I'll lade the way.   (*exeunt,* R.

SCENE SIXTII—*Sir Robert's parlor—Rose at table, stitching handkerchief.*

Rose.   It is almost time for Pat to be back—I sent him down to the village about two hours ago, for some worsted. I wonder how poor Charley is getting along—he must think it strange that I do not visit him; but then it is Patrick's fault, he always puts me off when I wish to go.

Pat. (*outside*) Git out o' that, ye ugly baste.

Rose.   There he is now. I thought he would never come.

Enter Pat, C.

My worsted, if you please.

Pat.   Yis, here it is, (*gives bundle*) an' I hope its the right kind.

Rose.   Why?

Pat.   Bekase I had to run all over the village for it.

Rose.   That doesn't matter much; but Pat, sit down, I wish to ask you a question.

Pat. (*seats himself—jumps up*) Och, murther! The divil take sich chairs, say I.

Rose.   What is the matter with the chair?

Pat. (*scratching head*) Faith, an' that's just f'what I'm afther tryin' to found out.

Rose.   Well, sit down.

Pat. (*sits on hard bottom chair*) I've always bin used to sitin' on benches, an' the loik o' that, an' not on sich fancy fixin's.

Rose.   Now, Pat, I want you to tell me what you were hinting at yesterday.

Pat.   Somethin I hinted at yesterday?

Rose.   Yes, you said: "never mind, I'll keep an eye on you, for I suspect that you are———." The rest I did not hear.

Pat.   Arrah, now, Miss, Rose, don't be afther mentionin' a poor divil's failin's.

Rose.   Now Patrick, that's a good fellow, tell me what you meant by those words.

Pat. (*aside*) The cunnin' little divil, she's afther soft-soapin' me. (*aloud*) I niver meant anythin' by thim words.

Rose You did, and you'll not tell me.   *(about to cry*

Pat. Don't cry, Miss Rose, an' I'll tell ye.

Rose. There, now you are a good fellow, after all.

Pat. Whist now, an' pay attention, as me ould captain used to say. On the day before yisterday, I wint to see me poor masther, an' we were talkin' about one thin' an' another, an' I says to him, says I: "masther, darlin', did ye murther the ould gintleman?" "No," says he. "Thin, masther, darlin," says I to him, says I, "I have an idea." "You have," says he to me. "Yis," says I. "Thin," says he to me, "let's have it," says he. "Masther, darlin," says I to him, "wouldn't ye loik to git out o' this?" "To be shure," says he to me, says he. An' wid that, we put our two heads togither, loik two peas in a pod, an' the consequence is that——

Rose. What, has he escaped?

Pat. No, he hasn't; but he has tex chances to one, o' gittin' out o' that dirthy hole, an' in two days more he'll be as free as aither you, or I.

Rose. Oh, thank you, and thank heaven, also. Oh, I'm so glad; but—but—but, you haven't told me what you meant by those mysterious words.

Pat. So ye want to know why I was speakin' to mesilf?

Rose. That's it exactly.

Pat. Well thin, me jewel, I niver mane f what I say, or say fwhat I mane.

Rose. And you will not tell me anything?

Pat. Faith, Miss Rose, I have nothin' to tell ye.

Rose. (*angrily*) Then you can go and attend to your own affairs. (*exit Pat, c.*) I know very well he means something. I wonder if he got the right kind of worsted. (*opens bundle*) There, now, I told him to get me red worst-and he has brought me yellow tape. But what is this. (*picks up paper*) Do my eyes deceive me? (*reads*) "Daring escape. The prisoner helped from outside. He undertakes to get out of a third-story window of the jail. The jailor discovers him in time. He cuts the rope which is tied in the cell. The prisoner is dashed to pieces on the prison yard. Last night, which, as all will remember, was a terrible one, one of the prisoners confined in the jail on the charge of murder—all will remember Charles——" Oh, heavens! how can I read more! "All will remember Charles Haliday, the young man who was convicted of the murder of Sir Robert Lancaster—conceived the idea of escaping by means of a rope, furnished by friends outside. He had tied the rope in his cell, and must have been half way down, when the jailor entered. Seeing, that on account of the storm, it would be worse than useless to raise an alarm, he quietly cut the rope. and the unfortunate young man was dashed—to—pieces—on—the—stones—with—which—the—prison—yard—is—paved. His—body—was—in—such—a—state—that—it—had—to—be—buried—immediately." Oh, heavens! dead, dead, and in a felon's grave!   *(sobs violently*

Enter Will, c.

Will. What, in tears! Why, my dear Miss Rose, what is the matter?

Rose. Nothing—I——excuse me.   *(exit c.*

Will. Now, I would like to know the reason of this agitation. (*reads paper, ad libitum*) So this then, is the cause of her agitation. Now the road is clear, and William Marlborough, if you do not win, you deserve a rope. I'll go and seek Ben. He will be able to arrange some plan; but who is this old man with Pat.

Enter Pat and Charles, R.

Pat. Here ye are now, Mr. Hobart. (*sees Will*) Where the divil's Miss Rose?

Will. She has just stepped to her room. Can I do anything for you?

Chas. No sir, I believe not.

Pat. I'll go an' see if me misthress will see ye, sur.

Chas. Thank you.   *(exit Pat, c.*

Will. You are a stranger a bout here, sir?

Chas. It has been some time since I was in this neighborhood.

Will. Then you do not know the current news.

Chas. Only that a young man named Haliday, had murdered Sir Robert Lancaster, and was in jail.

Will. (*handing paper*) And there you can read of his untimely end. I loved him as a brother, and to think that he should be such a scoundrel.

Chas. Then you believe him guilty.   (*takes spectacles from pocket*

Will. The proof against him was conclusive.

Chas. You were an eye witness?

Will. Not exactly; but I was the principal witness against him. I saw him bending over the body, knife in hand.

Chas. (*looking up from paper*) A horrible fate. Poor fellow, I pity him.

Will. So do I; but if he had taken my advice, he would not have died so early. If I am not too inquisitive, may I ask what you intend doing here?

Chas. Certainly. I heard that Miss Hazelwood needed a gardener, and as I am one, being rather hard up, I thought I would apply for the place.

Will. Success to you. I expect one of these days, to be——   .

Chas. What?

Will. That doesn't matter; but I must go and seek a friend of mine, so good day, and good luck to you, old man.

Chas. Thank you. (*exit William*, c.) The infernal villain—he little suspects who I am. So Haliday has found a grave within the prison walls. Good! This is some of Lynx's work. My greatest trial will come when I face Rose. She thinks me dead. Ah I hear some one approaching—It must be her.

Enter Rose and Pat—Charles pockets paper—Pat motions for silence.

Pat. Miss Rose, this is the ould gintleman, who has come to look afther the place, Andrew Hobart's his name.

Rose. You seem to be rather old for such work.

Chas. It is true, I am rather advanced in years; but I still have my strength.

Rose. Have you spoken to Patrick, about the terms.

Pat. He has, ma'am, an' he agrees to iverything.

Rose. Then you may take him to the kitchen, and give him a lunch, and then show him where he is to sleep.

Pat. All right, mam. Come along, ould man.

Chas. May the blessings of heaven rain down on you, for your kindness to me.   (*exit Charles and Pat*, c.

Rose. (*sinks into chair*) God knows that I need them, although you know it not, Mr. Hobart. Was ever a woman placed as I am—uncle murdered—lover dead, and buried in a prison yard. Ah, it is too much, too much!
                            (*buries face in hands*

Enter Will, c.

Will. I see, Miss Rose, that you have been made acquainted with news, which I would have kept from you: at least told you in such a manner that you would have been prepared for it. Rose, I love you, and it pains me to see you thus wasting yourself for a man who was unworthy of you.

Rose. He was not unworthy—he was innocent. I know it.

Will. But now that he is dead, will you be my wife?

Rose. I will promise to be your wife on two conditions.

Will. Name them.

Rose. The first is, that for the space of one year, you say nothing to me, whatever, of love or marriage.

Will. I promise—and the other condition?

Rose. That before three months, you clear the name of Charles Haliday, of the stain, which now rests upon it.

Will. But Rose, how——

Rose. You have hearu my conditions, accept or reject them, as you think proper.

Will. I accept your conditions.

Rose. Thank you—I will now retire.   (*exit*, c.

Will. Oh woman, woman! for you, I would murder my own brother. As it is I must give my dearest friend up; but how can I do it, without implicating myself? No matter, I have the proof.

Enter Jim, c.—*hides himself.*

I have the costume he wore, when he murdered Sir Robert. I told him that I had destroyed it; but I have it securely locked in my trunk. I must think it over.   (*exit*, c.—*Jim comes forward*

Jim. There is nothing like following up a fellow. I've been hunting around for three weeks to find that bloody rig. He's going to give his pardner up, is he? Well, I reckon I'll give em both up.

Enter Pat, c.

Pat. How are you, misther Jimmy?

Jim. How are you? How is Mr. Haliday?

Pat. Oh, he's all right.

Jim. Tell him that I would like to see him.

Pat. All right, Jimmy.   (*exit*, c.

Jim. How am I to get that trunk open—I've tried it a dozen times; but it won't be picked, and I can't get a duplicate key, because the lock is so hid that I can't get an impression of it, and I don't want to break it open, for then he would miss the rig at once, and leave the country,

Enter Charles and Pat, c.

and I don't want him to do that.

Chas. Don't want him to do what?

Jim. I don't want Mr. William Marlborough to leave the country. I know where that suit of old clothes is; but I don't know how to get it.

Chas. Where is it kept?

Jim. In a trunk, in his room. We might get out a warrant, arrest them, and search the premises; but I don't like to do that. I want to get all the proof in my hands first.

Chas. Yes, I should like to give them a surprise.

Jim. That's it exactly, so if you will wait a short time, I think I can manage it.

Chas. I am satisfied. Wait and watch, and if you can contrive to get this costume, well and good. If not we will adopt the other plan. (*exit Lynx,* c.)

Pat. An' if ye don't hurry up, I'll go an' git the ould thing, meself, so I will.

Chas. You wouldn't do anything without my consent, would you Pat?

Pat. Not unless I have to wait too long.

Chas. Well, come, let's go into the garden again.   (*exeunt*, c.

Enter Rose, R.

Rose. Mr. Marlborough promised a very difficult thing, still, if he does clear the name of Charles, from the dreadful stain upon it, no matter how much I despise the man, I will marry him.

Enter Jim, c.

Jim. Good morning.

Rose. Good morning; but I have not the pleasure of knowing your name.

Jim. My name, Miss Rose, is Jim Lynx, of the London Detective Force. I have been engaged to sift the murder case through.

Rose. Then Mr. Marlborough has commenced in earnest?

Jim. No ma'am, Mr. Marlborough does not know that I am here. I wish to have your permission, to have free access to your house at any and all times—do you grant it?

Rose. Yes sir.
Jim. Thank you. That is all. (*exit* c.
Rose. Everything grows so—so—I hardly know what. First I hear Pat use some mysterious words, then this detective, what did he mean. He is engaged on the—the—the murder of my uncle. What, oh what does all this mean! There is some mystery here, which I cannot fathom.

Enter Charles, c.

Chas. Ah, good morning. As the ground is too wet to work, I came in to read some of my favorite authors.
Rose. Any book, which you can find in the house, worthy of perusal, is at your disposal.
Chas. Thank you; but excuse an old man's inquisitiveness. I have been talking with Patrick, about you and Mr. Haliday. May I ask you a few questions?
Rose. Yes, any information, that I am posessed of, will be cheerfully given you.
Chas. I also wish to ask you a few questions, concerning yourself.
Rose. (*aside*) What can he mean? (*aloud*) You have my permission.
Chas. Does this Mr. Marlborough love you?
Rose. He says he does.
Chas. Do you love him?
Rose. I do not.
Chas. Do you still love Charles Haliday?
Rose. (*agitated*) I do.
Chas. It was proved in court that he was guilty of your uncle's murder.
Rose. My heart tells me he was innocent.
Chas. But then he is dead.
Rose. Yes, he is dead. (*aside*) Whenever this old man is near me I feel——
Chas. And knowing that he is dead, has not this Marlborough asked your hand in marriage?
Rose. He has.
Chas. And what was your answer?
Rose. I promised, on condition that he would, within three months, clear the name of Charles Haliday, from the foul stain which now rests upon it.
Chas. What if I were to tell you that he live?
Rose. Why, what do you mean, old man? Explain yourself—this suspense is terrible.
Chas. Then I tell you Charles Haliday lives.
Rose. Take me to him, for heaven's sake take me to him.
Chas. (*pulls off wig and whiskers*) Rose, he stands beside you.
Rose. (*falls in his arms*) Heaven, I thank thee.
Chas. Oh, Rose, Rose, my darling, I have looked forward to this meeting, with many misgivings; but thank heaven, I have found you true.
Rose. As if I could be otherwise; but how is it that you are alive, and all the papers say that you were killed?
Chas. The jailor must have invented it. As to how I escaped, I will tell you on another occasion.
Rose. And why not now, Charles?
Chas. Because I have a little surprise in store for you—you will wait?
Rose. Yes; but Charles, I have a question to ask you. Patrick was working around that immense moss rose bush, and by the merest chance in the world, I happened to go there. As I neared the bush, I overheard these words: "never mind, I'll keep my eye upon you, for I suspect you are——" His voice died away, and I could not hear the rest. (*starts*) What was that? I am sure I heard some one walking.
Chas. (*hastily putting on disguise*) I did not hear any one.

Rose. Come this way. *(they exit* R.

Enter Ben and Will, C.

Will. Now Ben, I have told you what her conditions are.

Ben. Well, the first condition is easy enough; but the second is not.

Will. No, it is not; but she is firm. If I do not clear Haliday in three months, she will not marry me.

Enter Jim, R.—*listening.*

Jim. (*aside*) Ah, ha, that's the reason you want to give your pardner away, is it?

Will. But this is not what I wished to talk to you about. Take a chair.

(sit down, Ben R.*, Will,* L. *of table*

Pat. (*at* L. *wing*) Och, the murtherin' villains, now we'll be afther hearin' some more bloody work.

Will. What do you think of this old man, who is employed here.

Ben. I think him a harmless old man ; but why?

Will. I suspect him. You read that article in the paper, of Haliday's daring attempt to escape, did you not?

Ben. Yes.

Will. It was not the jailor who cut that rope, it was your humble servant.

Pat advances, shaking stick, Jim points revolver, both return.

Ben. And so you suspect the old man.

Will. Precisely. I do not believe this tale about the burial of the prisoner; besides this old fellow has a peculiar way of looking at me, whenever I pass or speak to him.

Ben. I'll watch him.

Will. Do so. Now what do you advise.

Ben. In the girls case, nothing, as yet—as to the old man, watch him closely.

Will. There is another matter, I wish to speak to you about, as this one has been settled—this Irishman.

Pat. (*aside*) An' it's me, they're afther talkin' about. Faith, an' I'll be all ears. (*places ear outside scene*

Will. He has either found out something, or suspects too much.

Ben. Ah, I understand, you wish him——

Will. Exactly, I wish him out of the way.

Ben. How much do you consider the job worth?

Will. Just one thousand pounds.

Ben. In one week this Irishman will have ceased to exist. (*shake hands*) I must now go, and make my preparations.

Will. All right. I'll remain here, and perhaps I may catch a glimpse of my precious beauty. (*Ben exit* C., *followed by Lynx*) Ben has a close tongue, a cool head, and above all, he never quarrels about the price of a job, but still, if I wish to win Rose, I must give him up, and I'll do it. I will not allow any one to come between us.

Pat. (*aside*) Except Mr. Haliday, Jim Lynx an' yer humble sarvint.

Will. (*aside*) Did I not hear some one speak. Who's there? (*pause*) No answer. I'm getting very nervous of late. .

Enter Charles, C.

I am always imagining all sorts of things. (*Charles coughs—Will turns*) Good morning, Mr. Hobart. I was just wishing to see you, sir.

Chas. Then you will have your wish gratified, for here I am.

Will. You remember, in the last conversation we had, I asked you if you were a friend of Mr. Haliday?

Chas. I am a friend of Mr. Haliday.

Will. Then you have heard something, which in your mind, will shift the guilt on some one, and——

Enter Pat, suddenly, c.

Pat. Mr. Hobart, thim dirthy cows are in the garden again, atein' ivery blissed thing.

Will. (*aside*) I suspect him more and more.

Chas. As I was about to say, on no one can I bring my thoughts to rest as the guilty one, as I do not see the motive of the murder.

Will. Then you think there was a motive?

Chas. Most assuredly.

Will. And if you should find what the motive was, you will tell me?

Chas. Certainly I will.

Pat. Not.

Will. What did you say, Pat?

Pat. Faith, an' if I said anything it's mesilf don't know it.

Will. (*aside*) There is something in all this that I do not understand.

                                                        (*starts to go*)

Chas. You are not going?

Will. Yes. Just mention to Miss Rose that I was here, will you Pat?

Pat. I will. (*aside*) If I think of it.

Will. Now do not forget what you have promised, Mr. Hobart. (*exit*, c.)

Pat. That chap is afther suspectin' who ye are. masther darlin'. Take my advice, an' don't have much to say to him, will ye masther darlin'?

Chas. I promise you, Pat.

Enter Rose, R.

Rose. Who is it that has just left, Charles?

Pat. He tould me to tell ye, ma'am. It was Misther William Marlborough.

Rose. Oh! that hateful man—I wish he would not come so often.

Enter Lyux, c.

Jim. How do you all do?

Chas. First rate, Mr. Lynx—and you?

Jim. All right. (*aside to Pat*) I say, Pat, I want to have a word with you.

Pat. (*ditto*) Just wait awhile, an' ye may.

Chas. Come Rose, let's take a walk in the garden.   (*exeunt*, c.)

Pat. Now me honest detective, fwhat is it ye want to say to me.

Jim. It is this—I have found out the disguise that Ben has assumed, so when you leave the house, beware of an Irishman.

Pat. An' is it an Irishman, he'll be?

Jim. Yes.

Pat. Thanks, me friend, give us yer hand. (*shake hands*) I'll watch fer him, niver fear.

Jim. All right. (*going*) Tell your master that I have every thing ready and that in a short time, I am agoing to try and get that disguise.

Pat. An' may the howly St. Pathrick grant ye succiss. (*exit Jim*, c.) An' if there iver was an honest mon, that same is Jim Lynx, the detective. He has stuck to us, so he has, and I mane to stick to him. (*bell rings*) Ah, what is that?   (*exit R.*)

Enter Den and Will—sit at table, Will, R., *Ben*, L.

Ben. What does Miss Rose mean by these invitations, Will?

Will. I don't know; but there is something that I would like to know.

Ben. And what is that?

Will. What made you and I sleep so late.

Ben. Because we went to bed early; but softly, here comes Miss Rose.

Enter Rose c.

Rose. Good day, gentlemen.

Ben and Will. Good day.   (*Rose sits by Will, facing both*)

Ben. Miss Rose, I was astonished at receiving your kind note, and would

Rose. You are not astonished, are you Mr. Marlborough ?
Will. No ma'am, I am not.
Rose. We will talk of this later; but here comes Mr. Hobart.

Enter Charles, c.—sits between Ben and William, little in front of Ben.

Will. Good day, Mr. Hobart.
Chas. Same to you, sir.
Ben. Glad to see you, old man.
Chas. Thank you. Not interrupting the conversation in any manner, whatever, gentlemen, I would like to relate a strange dream, which I had last night.
Rose. What is it Mr. Hobart? Is it any thing dreadful?
Chas. I will leave that for you to say.
Will. Let's hear it by all means.
Chas. I think it will interest *you.*
Ben. (*aside*) What did he mean by speaking in that manner?
Chas. Well, to commence—but remember, it is only a dream.
Rose. Do proceed, Mr. Hobart—I am all curiosity.
Chas. I dreamed that there were two young men, who were close friends, at least so one of them thought—he had no secrets from the other, who appeared sincere. I dreamed that this young man, whose name was Charles, met a young lady, with whom he fell in love, as did his friend, also, and——
Ben. Here was the bone of contention?
Chas. Yes. Well, the pretended friend of Charles' soon found that he had no chance with the young lady. As soon as William found that he had been distanced by his friend, he went to work to devise some method of getting rid of his friend.
Will. And did he succeed?
Chas. Yes.
Ben. How did he do it?
Chas. He hired an assassin to do the work, which he, himself, dared not do. This young lady had an aged uncle, and this villain——
Rose. Hired a man to kill him?
Ben. (*agitated*) And did you dream how the murder was committed?
Chas. I did. The scene is before me, as plainly as if I had been an eye witness. I thought that this young man had just had a quarrel with this uncle; but they became friends again. (*Will and Ben look at each other*) They were in the parlor of the old gentleman, when in walked an old peddler, who was selling pictures. (*Ben clenches fists*

Enter Pat, L., quietly.

They bought one of him, and while they were examining the pictures, the wretch stole the knife, which this young man had in a——
Ben. Why, heaven! old man——
Chas. Be quiet. Remember I am only telling a dream.
Will. (*agitated*) Be quiet, Ben. What in the world is the matter with you?
Chas. Well, as I said before, this old wretch had stolen the knife which Charles carried, and no sooner had Charles left than——
Rose. The old peddler stabbed the uncle?
Chas. Precisely so, Miss Rose. Charles, hearing the cries of the old gentleman, rushed into the house, and there saw the old uncle lying on the floor, with a bloody knife by his side. He picked up the knife, recognized it as his own. He was horrified. He could not move. In this position he was surprised by his friend, who raised the cry of murder, and——
Will. He was taken to prison?
Chas. Yes, and not only taken to prison; but sentenced to remain there all his life.
Rose. Horrible.
Ben. And did your dream end there?
Chas. No it did not, there is a sequel.

Will. What is the sequel?

Chas. While in prison, he conceived the idea of escaping; but how to do it, was the question, as the cell in which he was confined, was in the third story of the building. At last however, by the aid of some friends, a rope was given him. He had already been furnished with a file, with which he had filed the bars nearly in two. He tied the rope on the opposite side of his cell, got out of the window, and when about half way down, this friend entered, and quick as thought, drew his knife and——

Will. Cut the rope.

Ben. And the poor fellow was dashed to pieces on the rocks below.

Chas. Not so.

Omnes. No?

Chas. The rope caught on something on the roof of one of the houses, and broke his fall.

Will. (*excitedly*) What do you mean?

Chas. I mean that your intended victim escaped you, villain that you are.

Will. (*jumps to his feet, Ben does also.*) You mean that——

Chas. (*jirks off beard etc.*) I am Charles Haliday.

Ben. (*draws knife*) If you escaped him, you will not escape me.

Ben attempts to stab Charles in back—Pat, rushes at Ben.

Pat. I'm at yer sarvice, ye murtherin' villain. (*hits him on head with stick—Ben falls*)

Enter Jim and police officer— Will runs, c.—fires at Charles—misses him—Jim shoots Will, who stagger, c.—Rose screams—throws herself in Charles' arms.

Will. I did all this for your sake, Rose. Farewell.   (*dies*

Chas. And may such be the death of every "False Friend." (*points at Will.*

PAT.   BEN.   CHARLES.   ROSE.   JIM.   POLICE OFFICER.
                       WILL.

CURTAIN.

To Our Customers.

Amateur companies frequently have trouble in procuring Plays well adapted to their wants, frequently ordering perhaps five dollars worth in single copies, before anything suitable can be found. All this can be done away with. Our catalogue embraces plays suitable for any and all companies, and if our friends will write to us, stating the requirments of their companies, there need be no trouble in this line, at least. If a temperanc society wants plays, we have something for them. If a company wants something which is very funny, we can suit them, In fact we have dramas, farces, comedies and tragedies, which *will* suit you. Enclose 15 cents per copy for as many sample copies as you may need, and we guarantee to suit you, if you will state the size of your company, and whether best adapted to the serious or funny. Give us a trial, at least.
                 A. D. AMES, Pub., Clyde, Ohio·

AMES' STANDARD AND MINOR DRAMA.

28. *THIRTY-THREE NEXT BIRTHDAY.* A Farce in one act, by John Madison Morton, 4 male, 2 female characters. Scene, outside of hotel, easily arranged. Costumes to suit the characters. This farce should be read to be appreciated, and is a good one as are all of Madison Morton's plays. The comedy characters are excellent. Time of performance, 35 minutes.

29. *THE PAINTER OF GHENT.* A Play in one act, by Douglass Jerrold, 5 male, 2 female characters. Scene in Ghent. Costumes of the country and period. This is a beautiful play of the tragic order. The character of the "Painter of Ghent," is one of grandeur and fine language. He becomes insane at the loss of children, and being a painter, paints their portraits from memory. A daughter whom he supposes dead, returns to him, and he recovers. A grand pley. Time of performance, 1 hour.

30. *A DAY WELL SPENT.* A Farce in one act, by John Oxenford, 7 male, 5 female characters. Scenery simple. Costumes, modern. Two clerks in the absence of their "boss" conclude to shut up shop, and have a spree. They get into several scrapes with the females, have numerous hair breadth escapes, and have a terrible time generally. Very amusing. Time of performance, 40 minutes.

31. *A PET OF THE PUBLIC.* A Farce in one act, by Edward Sterling, 4 male, 2 female characters. Scene, parlor. Costumes, modern. In this farce, the lady assumes four distinct characters, either of which is good. For an actress of versatility, it is a splendid piece, and amatuers can also produce it without trouble. It can either be used for a principal piece, or an afterpiece. Time of performance, 50 minutes.

32. *MY WIFE'S RELATIONS.* A Comedietta, in one act, by Walter Gordon, 4 male 4 female characters. Scene, plain apartments. Costumes, modern. A pleasing little piece well suited to amatuers, school exhibitions, etc. A fellow marries, her relatives comes to see her, are much more numerous than he has an idea of. The denoument is funny. Time of performance, 45 minutes.

33. *ON THE SLY.* A Farce in one act, by John Madison Morton, 3 male, 2 female characters. Scene, plain apartment. Costumes, modern. Husbands, don't never fall in love with your wife's dress makers—never squander your money foolishly, never do anything "on the sly," for your wives will be sure to find it out. This farce explains it all. Time of performance 45 minutes.

34. *THE MISTLETOE BOUGH.* A Melo Drama in two acts, by Charles Somerset, 7 male, 3 female characters. Scene, castle, chamber and wood. Costumes, doublets, trunks, etc. A most excellent Melo-Drama. Plenty of blood and thunder, with enough jolly, rollicking fun to nicely balance it. A great favorite with amatuers. Time of performance 1 hour and 30 minutes.

35. *HOW STOUT YOU'RE GETTING.* A Farce in one act, by John Madison Morton, 5 male, 2 female characters. Costumes, modern. Scene, a plain room. This is another of Morton's excellent farces. The comedy characters in it are nicely drawn, and it always is a favorite. Easily produced. Time of performance, 35 minutes.

36. *THE MILLER OF DERWENT WATER.* A Drama in three acts, by Edward Fitzball, 5 male, 2 female characters. Costumes, modern. Scenery, easily arranged. This is a touching little domestic drama, abounding in fine speeches, and appeals to the better feelings of one's nature. The "Miller" is an excellent old man. Two comedy characters keep the audience in good humor. Time of performance, 1 hour and 30 minutes.

37. *NOT SO BAD AFTER ALL.* A Comedy, in 3 acts, by Wybert Reeve 6 male, 5 female characters. Costumes, modern. Scenery, simple and easily arranged. Every character in this comedy is in itself a leading character, and every one very funny. Probably there is not a play in the language in which every character is so funny as this. Time of performance, 1 hour 40 minutes.

38. *THE BEWITCHED CLOSET.* A Sketch in one act, by Hattie Lena Lambla, 5 male, 2 female characters. Scene, Parson Grime's kitchen. Costumes modern. A lover goes to see his sweetheart, hides in a closet. Old man appears on the scene, thinks the closet bewitched. They upset it. Old man is frightened—runs away. Everything right etc. Time of performance, 15 minutes.

39. *A LIFE'S REVENGE.* A Drama in 3 acts, by Wm. E. Suter, 7 males, 5 female characters. Costumes, French, period 1661. Scenery, palace, gardens, prison. Can be arranged by amatuers but is a heavy piece. A fine leading man, heavy man, a glorious comedy, etc. Also leading lady, juvenile lady, comedy lady, etc. This drama was a favorite with Harold Forsberg. Time of performance, 2 hours and 15 minutes.

40. *THAT MYSTERIOUS BUNDLE.* A Farce in one act, by Hattie Lena Lambla. 2 male, 2 female characters. Costumes, modern. Scenery, a plain room. A Variety peice, yet can be performed by Amatuers, etc. A Mysterious bundle figures in this farce, which contains a——. Time of performance, 20 minutes.

41. *WON AT LAST.* A Comedy Drama in 3 acts, by Wybert Reeve, 7 male, 3 female characters. Costumes modern. Scenery, drawing-room, street and office. Every character is good. Jennie Hight starred on the character of "Constance" in this play. Amatuers can produce it. Time of performance, 1 hour 45 minutes.

42. *DOMESTIC FELICITY.* A Farce in one act, by Hattie Lena Lambla, 1 male, 1 female character. Costumes modern. Scene, a dining room. The name fully describes the piece. Very funny. Time of performance, fifteen minutes.

43. *ARRAH DE BAUGH.* A Drama in 5 acts, by F. C. Kinnaman, 7 male, 5 female characters. Costumes modern. Scenes, exteriors and interiors. A most exquisite love story in a play, abounding in scenes of great beauty. The depth of woman's love is beautifully shown. Time of performance about two hours.

44. *OBEDIENCE, OR TOO MINDFUL BY FAR.* A Comedietta in one act, by Hattie Lena Lambla, 1 male, 2 female characters. Costumes modern. Scenes, plain room and bed room. An old fellow who thinks he is very sick, becomes vely peevish and particular. A plot is formed to break him of his foolishness. Very amusing. Time of performance twenty minutes.

45. *ROCK ALLEN THE ORPHAN, OR LOST AND FOUND.* A Comedy Drama in one act, by W. Henri Wilkins, 5 male, 3 female characters. Costumes modern. Scenes interiors. Time, during the Rebellion. This play represents the real "deown east" characters to perfection. An old man and woman are always quarreling, and their difficulties are very amusing. Time of performance, one hour and twenty minutes.

46. *MAN AND WIFE.* A Drama in five acts, by H. A. Webber, 12 male, 7 female characters. Costumes modern. Scenery exteriors and interiors. This drama is one of intense interest and is a faithful dramatization of Wilkie Collins' story of the same name. This is said by competant critics to be the best dramatization published, and it should be in the hands of every dramatic company in the country. It has become a great favorite.

47. *IN THE WRONG BOX.* An Ethiopean Farce in one act, by M. A. D. Clifton, 3 male characters. Costumes, peddler's and darkey's dilapidated dress. Scene, a wood. Characters represented, a darkey, an Irishman and a Yankee. Time of performance twenty minutes.

48. *SCHNAPPS.* A Dutch Farce in one act, M. A. D. Clifton, 1 male, 1 female character. Costumes, burlesque German. Scene, a plain room. A neat little piece for two Dutch players, introducing songs and dances. Time of performance, 15 to 30 minutes, at the pleasure of the performers.

49. *DER TWO SUBPRISES.* A Dutch Farce in one act, by M. A. D. Clifton, 1 male, 1 female character. Costumes, peasant's, and old man's and old woman's dress. Scene, a kitchen. A very neat little sketch, introducing songs and dances. Time of performance, about twenty minutes.

50. *HAMLET.* A Tragedy in five acts, by Shakespeare, 15 male, 3 female characters. Probably no other play by the immortal Shakespeare is produced as frequently as this one. It needs no description. Time of performance about two hours and thirty minutes.

51. *RESCUED.* A Temperance Drama in two acts, by Clayton H. Gilbert, 5 male, 3 female characters. This play visibly depicts the dangerous consequences of falling into bad company, the follies of the intoxicating bowl, and shows that even the pure love of a noble girl will be sacrificed to the accursed appetite. The solemn scenes are balanced by the funny portions, and all in all the play is a grand success. Costumes modern. Scenes, interiors some neatly and some handsomely furnished. Time of performance one hour.

52. *HENRY GRANDEN.* A Drama in three acts, by Frank Lester Bingham, 11 male, 8 female characters. This drama is sensational in a high degree, abounding in thrilling scenes among the Indians, hair breadth escapes, etc. It should be purchased by every dramatic company that wish something to suit the public. Costumes not hard to arrange. Time of performance two hours.

53. *OUT IN THE STREETS.* A Temperance Drama in three acts, by S. N. Cook, 6 male, 4 female characters. Wherever this drama has been produced it has been received with the greatest enthusiasm. Listeners have been melted to tears at the troubles of Mrs. Bradford, and in the next scene been convulsed with laughter at the drolleries of North Carolina Pete. Costumes modern. Scenes, interiors. Time of performance, about one hour.

54. *THE TWO T. J's.* A Farce in one act, by Martin Beecher, 4 male, 2 female characters. Costumes of the day ; scene an ordinary room. This is a capital farce and has two male characters excellent for light and low comedians. Good parts also for old and young lady. Time of performance thirty minutes.

55. *SOMEBODY'S NOBODY.* A Farce in one act and one scene, by C. A. Maltby, 3 male, 2 female characters. Scene, interior. Easily arranged 'n any parlor or hall, as it can be produced without scenery. Costumes modern with the exception of Dick Mizzle's which is hostler's and afterwards extravagant fashionable. This most laughable farce was first produced at the Drury Lane Theater, London, where it had a run of one hundred and fifty consecutive nights. It is all comic, and has excellent parts for old man, walking gent, low comedy, walking lady and chambermaid. Time of performance, 30 minutes.

56. *WOOING UNDER DIFFICULTIES.* A Farce in one act and one scene, by John T. Douglass, 4 male, 3 female characters. Scene, handsomely furnished apartment. Costumes of the day. Probably no poor fellow ever wooed under more distressing difficulties than the one in this farce. It all comes about through a serious misunderstanding. A crusty old man, and a quarrelsome and very important servant go to make the farce extremely funny. Time of performance thirty minutes.

57. *PADDY MILES' BOY.* An Irish Farce in one act, by James Pilgrim, 5 male, 2 female characters. Scenes, exteriors and interiors. Costumes eccentric, and Irish for Paddy. Probably there is not an Irish farce published so often presented as this one, but it is always a favorite and is always received with great applause. Time of performance 35 minutes.

58. *WRECKED.* A Temperance play in two acts, by A. D. Ames, 9 male, 3 female characters. Scenes, drawing room, saloon, street and jail. Costumes modern. The lessons learned in this drama are most excellent. The language is pure, containing nothing to offend the most refined ear. From the comfortable home and pleasant fireside, it follows the downward course of the drunkard to the end. All this is followed by counterfeiting, the death of the faithful wife caused by a blow from the hand of a drunken husband, and finally the death of the drunkard in the madhouse. Time of performance about one hour.

59. *SAVED.* A Temperance Sketch in two acts, by Edwin Tardy, 2 male, 3 female characters. Scenes, street and plain room. Nicely adapted to amatuers, Time of performance twenty minutes.

60. *DRIVEN TO THE WALL, OR TRUE TO THE LAST.* A Play in four acts, by A. D. Ames. 10 male and 3 female characters. For beauty of dialogue, startling situations, depths of feeling there is none on the American Stage superior to this one. The plot is an exceedingly deep one, and the interest begins with the first speech, and does not for a moment cease until the curtain falls on the last scene of the last act. The cast is small and the costumes easily arranged. It can be played on any stage. It has parts for Leading Emotional Lady, Juvenile Lady, Leading Man, Villain, Character Old Man. First Old Man, Comedy, etc.

61. *NOT AS DEAF AS HE SEEMS.* An Ethiopean Farce in one act. 2 male characters. Scene, a plain room. Costumes exagerated and comic. Extremely ridiculous and funny. Time of performance 15 minutes.

62. *TEN NIGHTS IN A BAR-ROOM.* A Temperance Play in five acts, by Wm. W. Pratt, from T. S. Arther's novel of the same name—7 male, 3 female characters. This edition is rewritten, containing many new points, and is the best ever presented to the public. Nothing need be said in its praise, as it is too well known. It is often played, and always successfully. Time of performance about two hours.

63. *THREE GLASSES A DAY,* Or, The Broken Home. A grand Moral and Temperance Drama, in two acts, by W. Henri Wilkins, 4 male, 2 female characters. Costumes modern. Scenes, interiors. First-class characters for Leading Man, Villain, a genuine down-east Yankee, which is also very funny ; also Leading Lady, and a tip-top Comedy Lady. If a company wishes something with an excellent moral, at the same time running over with genuine humor, buy this. Time of performance about one hour and thirty minutes.

64. *THAT BOY SAM.* An Ethiopian Farce in one act, by F. L. Cutler. 8 male, 1 female character. Scene, a plain room and common furniture. Costumes, comic, to suit the characters. Very funny, and effectually gives the troubles of a "colored gal" in trying to have a beau, and the pranks of "that boy Sam." Time of performance twenty minutes.

65. *AN UNWELCOME RETURN.* A Comic Interlude, in one act, by Geo. A. Munson. 3 male, 1 female character. Scene, a dining room. Costumes. modern. Companies will find this a very amusing piece, two negroes being very funny—enough so to keep an audience in the best of humor. Time of performance, twenty minutes.

66. *HANS, THE DUTCH J. P.* A Dutch Farce in one act, by F. L. Cutler, 3 male, 1 female character. An exceedingly funny piece. Hans figures as a Justice in the absence of his master, and his exploits are extremely ludicrous. Costumes modern. Scene, plain room. Time of performance, twenty minutes.

67. *THE FALSE FRIEND.* A Drama in two acts, by Geo. S. Vautrot. 6 male, 1 female character. Simple scenery and costumes. First class characters for leading man, old man, villain, a rollicking Irishman, etc. also a good leading lady. This drama is one of thrilling interest, and dramatic companies will invariably be pleased with it. Time of performance, one hour and forty-five minutes.

68. *THE SHAM PROFESSOR.* A Farce in one act, by F. L. Cutler. 4 male characters. This intensely funny afterpiece can be produced by any company. The characters are all first class, and the "colored individual" is especially funny. Scene, a plain room. Costumes, simple. Time of performance, about twenty minutes.

69. *MOTHER'S FOOL.* A Farce in one act, by W. Henri Wilkins. 6 male, 1 female character. Like all of Mr. Wilkins' plays, this is first class. The characters are all well drawn, it is very amusing, and proves an immense success wherever produced. Scene, a simple room. Costumes modern. Time of performance, thirty minutes.

70. *WHICH WILL HE MARRY.* A Farce in one act, by Thomas Egerton Wilks. 2 male, 8 female characters. Scene, a street. Costumes modern. Easily arranged on any stage. A barber hears that one of eight women has fallen heir to some money, not knowing which, he makes love to them all. This, together with the revenge the females have upon him, will prove laughable enough to suit any one. Time of representation, thirty minutes.

71. *THE REWARD OF CRIME, OR THE LOVE OF GOLD.* A Drama of Vermont, in two acts. by W. Henri Wilkins. 5 male, 3 female characters. A drama from the pen of this author is sufficient guarantee of its excellence. Characters for old man, 1st and 2d heavy men, juvenile. A splendid Yankee, lively enough to suit any one. Old woman, juvenile woman, and comedy. Costumes modern. Scene, plain rooms and street. Time of performance, one hour and thirty minutes. Easily placed upon the stage, and a great favorite with amatuers.

72. *THE DEUCE IS IN HIM.* A Farce in one act, by R. J. Raymond. 5 male, 1 female character. Scene, a plain room. Costumes modern. This farce is easily arranged, and can be produced on any stage, in fact, in a parlor. The pranks of the doctor's boy will keep an audience in roars of laughter, every line being full of fun. Time of performance, thirty minutes. Order this, and you will be pleased.

73. *AT LAST.* A Temperance Drama in three acts, by G. S. Vautrot. 7 male 1 female character. This is one of the most effective temperance plays ever published. Good characters for leading man, 1st and 2d villain, a detective, old man, a Yankee, and a capital negro, also leading lady. The temptations of city life are faithfully depicted, the effects of gambling, strong drink, etc. Every company that orders it will produce it. Costumes modern. Scene, Mobile. Time of performance, one hour and thirty minutes.

74. *HOW TO TAME YOUR MOTHER-IN-LAW.* A Farce in one act, by Henry J. Byron. 4 male, 2 female characters. Scene, parlor, supposed to be in the rear of a grocers shop. Costumes modern. Whiffles the proprietor of the grocery, has a mother-in-law who is always interfering with his business. Various expedients are resorted to to cure her—a mutual friend is called in who, by the aid of various disguises frightens the old lady nearly to death, finally Whiffles gets on a "ge-lorious drunk," and at last triumphs. A perfect success. Time of performance, thirty-five minutes.

www.ingramcontent.com/pod-product-compliance
Lightning Source LLC
Chambersburg PA
CBHW061237260626
47172CB00003B/892